LILY'S
PROMISE

LILY'S PROMISE

KATHRYN ERSKINE

Quill Tree Books
An Imprint of HarperCollinsPublishers

Quill Tree Books is an imprint of HarperCollins Publishers.

Lily's Promise
Copyright © 2021 by Kathryn Erskine
www.harpercollinschildrens.com

Library of Congress Control Number: 2020952876
ISBN 978-0-06-305815-6

Typography by Laura Mock
21 22 23 24 25   PC/LSCH   10 9 8 7 6 5 4 3 2 1

First Edition

To you, smart reader,
with respect and best wishes
as you create your own life story

Day One

$\mathcal{L}$ily stands, facing the crowd of kids. She wants nothing more than to turn and run. The dress she chose so carefully now makes her feel conspicuous, as if she stepped into J. H. Banning Upper Elementary from a different century. She picks at the charm bracelet on her left wrist. Dad said it would bring her good luck, but it feels like a heavy chain. Even pressing the Labradoodle charm between her thumb and forefinger, hard enough to leave an imprint, isn't helping.

She hears her own breathing, louder than the buzz in the cafeteria. And she smells the mixture of gravy and spray cleaner and wet that permeates the place. She thinks she might throw up.

Hobart stands behind her. He chews his lip, moving his

mouth enough to wiggle his tartan bow tie. His skinny arms that dangle from a short-sleeved shirt are stuck stiffly by his sides, then folded tightly against his chest, repeatedly. He's alternately hot and cold and wishes his body would make up its mind. And he wants to jump and yell, "*In* the *house!*" but knows this isn't the time.

He looks out at the crowd, willing them to be kind.

Libro

I suspect you think that "Day One" is the beginning of the story. Understandable error. Let me point out that just because it's the first page does not mean it's the beginning.

Every book has a backstory. You will never see it because it started even before the first page, but if the Imaginer does a good job, the characters will feel like real people . . . because they are. They're out there somewhere. Maybe one of them is you. Or they're imagined. But imagination is real. Without it, we wouldn't have any of the great inventions. You wouldn't be holding this story in any format—paper or electronic or audio. Where would we be without imagination? Without wonder?

Maybe you're wondering who I am, what character I am

in this book. And why I have all the answers. I don't. I'm limited by bookends. Literally. I am the book. That's right. The book. The vessel. The holder, carrier of the story. I know some things you don't because I know the Imaginer who is writing this—fairly well but not everything that goes on in that dense, twisted mind.

I know more than you because of what the Imaginer spilled onto my pages and then rephrased or trimmed or cut altogether. Sometimes those are the most interesting bits. Or funny, or frightening, or thought-provoking. But they're gone without any approval from me. I have no voice.

That's why I'm jealous of you. Yes, jealous. I may know more than you, what has come and gone, and when, and even why, but I am only a static vessel. A receiver. I make none of the choices.

But you? You make choices every day. And every choice has a consequence—in real life, and in a story. You have complete control over your thoughts and actions. As you get older, you'll have even more. Me, I will still be stuck between the covers.

Sigh.

Do books sigh?

I just did.

So yes, obviously.

As I was saying, my thoughts, my feelings, my ideas, are all given to me. Or are they? Sometimes I do run away with the story. Usually I'm caught. But not always.

I invite you to accompany me on this journey. Let us bear witness together, smart reader. Why do I call you "smart" reader? I know, it is redundant. Obviously, if you're reading, you're smart already. Think of it as a reminder.

Ah, I hear the Imaginer's footsteps coming up the stairs to the attic, so we must return to Lily and Hobart.

Incidentally, Hobart? Really? With a tartan bow tie. Who does that? I do wonder about the Imaginer sometimes . . . no, often.

Chapter 1

"Hi! I'm Hobart!" The boy spoke loudly enough that Lily startled and took a step back. It was noisy in the cafeteria, but did he really have to shout?

"Sorry!" Hobart said.

Lily wondered if he always spoke in shouts. It made her whisper, to even things out. "I'm Lily."

"I know!"

Lily tried not to shudder at the shouting that felt like a shove.

"I'm supposed to show you around because you're new!"

"Oh." Lily hadn't thought of that possibility. As a home-schooler, there was never a need for that. She looked around the mass of students. "I didn't know they did that in schools."

"Oh, it's not a school thing. My mom told me to. You're the new kid in my homeroom, and your mom is a professor, so she says that means you're probably really smart. Are you?"

"Um . . . I—I guess so."

Hobart frowned. "That doesn't sound very smart."

"Well, it's awkward to be asked if you're really smart because if you say yes then you sound conceited," Lily found herself explaining, which surprised her because normally she'd only think a response in her head.

"Oh, I get it! Awkward is my middle name." Hobart smiled. "Not really, that's just what my dad says."

A three-tone chime sounded, followed by an amplified voice saying, "You may now proceed to your homeroom classes. Welcome to the first day of school!"

"Cool! I'll show you where—" Hobart started, but a tall sandy-haired boy in a hockey jersey walked into him, knocking him hard against a cafeteria table.

"Hi, Ho-*fart*!" The boy put his forearm to his mouth and made a farting sound before announcing, loudly, "I heard Ho-fart has a medical condition that makes him fart all the time! I feel sorry for him." He pushed into the crowd of kids leaving the cafeteria, followed by a group of guffawing boys.

Hobart laughed it off with a shrug.

"That was mean," Lily whispered.

"It's okay. I figure if he has me to pick on then he'll leave other kids alone." Hobart's face brightened into a grin. "Come on! I'll take you to homeroom!"

Lily couldn't help but smile, not about the bullying. That bothered her. A lot. What made her smile was that Hobart was so kind and maybe, just maybe, she'd found a friend. She didn't really know how to make a friend on her own—she'd been thrown in with other kids for home-schooling events, and sometimes she'd played with a group of kids in her old neighborhood, but actually finding and making a friend herself? She wasn't sure she could. And almost worse than that, she wasn't sure she knew how to be a good friend . . . other than to Skippy.

As she followed Hobart down the scarily noisy, crowded corridor, she thought about how Dad had always encouraged her to talk with other kids. *Girls make excellent friends*, he'd said. She wondered if Dad would've said boys make excellent friends, too.

Libro

See? I bet you were wondering about that Hobart, just like I was, initially. But names, and looks, can be deceiving. I've grown to like Hobart a lot. Even if his father says Awkward is his middle name. That is not a fair identifier. The Imaginer says my middle name is Snarky. How she glommed on to such a ludicrous notion, I have no idea.

I am not fond of that boy who shoved Hobart. And making flatulent sounds? What is this, elementary school? Oh. Yes, I suppose it is, but the Imaginer did say J. H. Banning Upper Elementary, and I happen to know that these particular children are sixth graders. I find that boy's behavior rather immature for sixth grade . . . although I know some of you are thinking of making, and perhaps actually making, some of those noises right now.

Moving on.

Who is Lily's friend, Skippy? Let us hope that Lily's only friend to date has not been a jar of peanut butter.

Chapter 2

Hobart led Lily into a classroom that, if anything, was louder than the cafeteria. A young woman stood by a desk at the front of the room, one hand gripping the edge, the other hand clutching a scarf at her throat. She was addressing the class but kept getting drowned out.

"I'm Miss Chase . . .

"I know you all are excited . . .

"I know it's the first day . . .

"Could you please quiet down a bit?"

Nothing stopped the din, until a woman the age of Lily's mom stuck her head in the classroom. "People! What is going on in here? Let's show some respect." The room quieted substantially. "In your seats. Now. Thank you."

By the time she'd finished saying "Thank you," she

was speaking in a normal tone of voice and everyone who wasn't already in a seat was heading there.

Lily found herself wishing this woman were her teacher. Especially when, after the brief, blissful calm of the Pledge of Allegiance, Miss Chase said, "Lily, you and I are new to this school. Why don't you introduce yourself?"

All eyes were on Lily now and she felt her face grow hot. She hadn't prepared for this. It was hard to swallow and she needed to because her throat was so dry. What was she supposed to say? *Hi, I was homeschooled until now? Then my dad died. He was the best teacher anyone could ever . . .* She felt herself tearing up.

"She's really smart!" Hobart piped up from the desk next to her.

The boy who'd knocked into Hobart in the cafeteria snorted from the back of the room. "How would you know? She's mute." Several boys around him giggled.

Miss Chase pointed to the sign above the whiteboard in the front of the room. Respect Is Our Cornerstone. "Remember we want to respect each other, right?"

Lily wondered why she said it as a question.

The girl in front of Lily turned in her seat, flipped her hair, and ran the heart on her gold necklace back and forth over the chain. "Hi, Lily, I'm Ava, and"—she pointed to the girl at the desk next to her—"this is Samantha. I like your dress. We started a fashion club if you want to join."

A fashion club? Lily liked wearing dresses but only because they were comfortable. She wasn't particularly interested in fashion. At all. Still, here was a girl trying to be nice and she knew Mom would say to accept the invitation.

She hesitated too long. Ava and Samantha looked at each other, their eyebrows raised. "So . . . if you change your mind," Ava said, "let us know."

Ava didn't look like she expected Lily to change her mind. In fact, she looked at Lily as if she were a snob. *I'm not a snob*, Lily wanted to say, *I'm just shy.*

Homeroom morphed into math class. In the same room. With the same teacher. Which meant there wasn't much math happening.

The boy who'd pushed Hobart in the cafeteria peppered Miss Chase with questions about the upcoming student council election, which Miss Chase had tried to talk about in the fifteen-minute block before math, except the boy hadn't seemed interested at that point.

Lily learned that his name was Ryan because a girl with spiked pink hair who sat in the front row periodically muttered, "Stop it, Ryan," or "It's math now, Ryan."

Miss Chase kept looking at her watch and saying, "We really should focus on math," and "We're running out of time . . ." until the tones rang, signifying it was time for the next class.

"That was painful," Hobart said, as they were carried along the hallway by the mass of students. "What class do you have next?"

Lily looked at her schedule, even though she'd memorized it. "Social studies."

"I have PE," Hobart said, looking over her shoulder, "but I see you have 'A' lunch so we can sit together!"

Lily smiled. That solved her second greatest fear about school, after making friends: cafeteria hazards.

Lily walked into her classroom and was instantly pleased. The good news about social studies class was the teacher: Mrs. Barry, the very same teacher who'd stuck her head in Miss Chase's class to quiet everyone down. The bad news was the students: Ryan, the bully, and his gang of followers.

"Welcome, everyone!" Mrs. Barry said. She smiled at Lily and several other students. "We have some newcomers . . ." She paused and Lily thought, *Please, please, please, don't make me introduce myself*, but Mrs. Barry simply said, "So I hope you'll work on making everyone feel welcome."

Ryan snorted from the back of the room.

"Yes, that means you, too, Ryan."

Lily breathed a sigh of relief and even had to suppress a smile as several kids said, "Ooooh."

Mrs. Barry pointed to a shoebox on a small table by the classroom door. "Lastly, put your phones in the box!"

"Why can't we just put them in sleep mode?" Ryan grumbled.

"Because your phones have a habit of waking up when they're with you because you people are so interesting!" She winked and several kids laughed. With some reluctance, everyone put their phones in the shoebox.

"Lily?" Mrs. Barry said, giving a nod to the box of phones.

"I don't have one," Lily said quietly.

Ryan hooted. "What kind of person doesn't have a phone?"

"A person who's not distracted," Mrs. Barry said, glaring at Ryan.

Lily hadn't needed a phone before. She'd always been with Dad. And even now, Mom didn't believe in phones because it took kids away from communicating with people face-to-face. Mom didn't like social media, in general, because kids could say very hurtful things without even thinking. "What about when I'm in middle school?" Lily had asked. "*Especially* not in middle school," Mom had said.

As class began, Lily noticed that everyone paid attention to Mrs. Barry. Students were talking, but they were talking about immigration, specifically the countries from which students at J. H. Banning Upper Elementary School had emigrated. Mrs. Barry broke them into groups and each one had a different country. Lily's group was assigned Syria.

She looked at the two other kids at her table. One was a small, scruffy boy with matted blond hair she recognized from homeroom. He kept his head down and twirled a chewed pencil in his hands. The other was a girl who was too busy drawing on herself and admiring her work to have much interest in conversation, other than to say, "We're both named after flowers." Lily didn't know how to start the conversation and didn't like trying to start them, anyway.

Mrs. Barry walked from group to group, laying a bunch of granola bars on each table. "No nuts, gluten, or dairy in these bars."

She paused at their table. "Lovely artwork, Iris. Now let's focus on discussing your topic."

Next, she looked at the boy, who swung his legs back and forth without touching the floor. His wrinkled, white T-shirt hung off his small frame. He was staring at the granola bars.

"Skylar?" Mrs. Barry said.

The boy froze and his eyes widened.

"I know you have good ideas. Let's share them. You, too, Lily," she said with a smile.

Lily heard Dad's voice in her head, saying the same thing. *You have good ideas, Lily. You just need to share them.* He'd told her that if her ideas stayed inside her head, no one would ever know, and eventually she'd feel unheard and insignificant. *If something is important to you, you* have *to speak up.*

Still, no one at her table, including Lily, spoke. Iris simply pushed the pile of granola bars to Skylar. He glanced from Lily to the bars, then back to Lily.

"I don't want any, thanks," she said.

She watched as he gently laid his pencil down and reached for the granola bars like they were a treasure. He didn't just throw them in his backpack. He made a nest for them in a sweatshirt that was stuffed inside, then put the arms of the sweatshirt over top of the granola bars before zipping up his backpack.

"Let's stay on topic, people." Mrs. Barry clapped her hands, startling Lily, and making her realize she'd been staring at Skylar. She quickly looked at Mrs. Barry. "I'm starting to hear sidebar conversations, and while the latest film releases are interesting, unless they're being shown in the countries you're discussing, they're not pertinent."

"What if they *are* being shown there?" Ryan said.

"Then I want to know where the movie theaters are, what languages the subtitles might be in, what people are wearing, and who is allowed to attend."

Ryan started to speak, but Mrs. Barry held her hand up. "Focus, Ryan. We're sharing what we've learned in fifteen minutes."

Skylar was back to fiddling with his pencil, spurring

Lily to take out a pen and piece of paper. She began writing down all the information she knew about Syria. She'd heard her parents discuss the refugee camps and the war that had raged for many years. From studying for the National Geographic GeoBee with her dad, she also knew the capital was Damascus and the official language was Arabic but there were many more spoken, like Kurdish, French, and English, along with some others she couldn't remember. The official religion was Islam, most people being Sunni Muslims, although there were a variety of other religions, including Christianity. The Kurdish minority mostly lived in the north near the border with Turkey and Iraq. They were supposed to get their own country after World War I, but they never did. She finished by writing, "The Kurds are discriminated against, which isn't fair."

When she slid the sheet of paper to the middle of their table, Iris raised her eyebrows but kept drawing. Skylar leaned forward, elbows on the table, to read what Lily had written. After nodding, he leaned back, and the three of them remained silent while the groups around them talked.

Lily clutched her charm bracelet. She felt guilty. She wasn't living up to Dad's Strive for Five challenge. And she'd promised him. Writing something down didn't count. She was already good at that.

Dad had wanted Lily to speak up, make herself heard, step out of her "comfort zone," at least five times and then she'd see, according to him, that the sixth time was easier, the seventh even easier, and pretty soon, it would become second nature. She found that hard to believe, although she had to admit that he was usually right, like when he forced her to try things that she 97 percent didn't want to do but had to admit that 3 percent of her did. . . . Well, she ended up liking them. Still, she couldn't imagine enjoying speaking up. Ever.

Besides, the challenge was called *Strive* for Five. So *trying* counted; she didn't actually have to speak. Except, if she were being honest, she wasn't even trying. Not really.

She'd rather listen and observe. In fact, Lily found herself trying to eavesdrop on the conversation at a neighboring table where a girl in a headscarf sat, an *English for Everyone* book in front of her. Maybe she was an immigrant? Or maybe she was helping tutor immigrants?

"Okay, everyone. Let's wrap up the discussion," Mrs. Barry said, stopping to pick up Lily's paper. She read the first few lines. "Impressive. How did you all come up with this? Given that you have no tablets or books on your table."

Skylar quickly pointed his finger at Lily, then put his hand back in his lap.

"Lily? Do you have a special interest in Syria?"

Lily swallowed, and when she tried to speak her voice cracked. She cleared her throat and tried again. "I was studying for GeoBee."

"What's that?" Iris said.

"The National Geographic geography bee. It's like a spelling bee, only it's facts about geography."

"Interesting," Mrs. Barry mused, still looking at the paper before putting it down on their table. "Okay, class! Let's share what we've learned." She raised her eyebrows at Lily.

Lily quickly looked down at the table. Fortunately, another girl volunteered, and several more kids after her, so Lily's group didn't have to. Still, she could feel Mrs. Barry's eyes on her.

At the end of class, as students filed out, Lily was zipping up her backpack and hoisting it on her shoulder.

"Didn't you get a locker?" Mrs. Barry asked. "You don't have to carry your backpack around all day."

"I don't mind," Lily said quickly, clutching the strap. It held a copy of Dad's letter, the original safe at home, just in case. It was like having her dad with her all the time.

Mrs. Barry nodded. "Would you be interested if we started a GeoBee club here?"

Lily gave a lukewarm "Maybe," since it seemed rude to say no. But she didn't want to do the bee. Dad had already tried to get her to compete.

"Think about it, and in the meantime, if you have questions or any issues crop up, feel free to talk with me." She smiled. "I've been here a long time, so I know the scoop."

Lily wanted to ask her if she could teach Miss Chase's class for her or if she could stop Ryan from being a bully to Hobart, but she was pretty sure that wasn't what Mrs. Barry meant. She probably meant answering questions like where's the restroom, and what classes to sign up for in middle school. Lily simply whispered, "Thank you," and clutched her book, *Amal Unbound*, which she'd brought in case she had to eat lunch alone, as she headed for the cafeteria to find Hobart.

Libro

I like Lily already. Anyone who loves books is a friend of mine. Also, smart, wise, and interesting. Spending time with books (ahem, such as myself) has a way of doing that for people.

Question: Is anyone going to do something about Ryan? I do not care for that character. Is he the nemesis in the story? Every book has to have a "bad guy."

Hint: I am not the "bad guy." Sometimes mildly misbehaved but certainly nothing like Ryan.

Trust me.

You'll see.

Chapter 3

$\mathcal{L}$ ily wove her way through the kids in the hall as lockers slammed and voices shouted around her. The pale green walls matched the linoleum floor and, together with the gray lockers, made the hallway feel depressing and Lily's stomach somewhat unsettled. She was grateful to finally reach the cafeteria.

Unfortunately, she couldn't find Hobart. She searched the cafeteria and noticed the posters on the wall, one saying J. H. Banning Students Show Respect, and several about throwing food: Food Fights Aren't Right! and NO Throwing Food! and Apples Are for Eating. Balls Are for Throwing! Underneath the last one, someone had added words in bold, black Sharpie: NO Throwing Balls in the Cafeteria, Either!

Lily felt sick. She had worried about the noise, the smell, the need to find a place to sit, and possibly even having to talk with people, but dodging food? She hadn't counted on that.

She grabbed a tray and got in line. None of the food looked appetizing and the cafeteria smelled nothing like her kitchen at home. She selected a wrapped salad and some cheese sticks. Tomorrow she was definitely bringing her lunch. Clutching her tray, she walked up and down the rows of tables. She saw some girls sitting at one table, talking and laughing, but she was too shy to go over and try, "Hi! Can I sit with you?" like her mother suggested. Her mom could do something like that. It was how she'd met Lily's dad, who had been quiet and shy, like Lily.

There were lots of groups of kids and she wished she could be a part of one, but her voice just wouldn't come out, except with Hobart. She had the feeling that she didn't have to worry about anything she said around Hobart. He'd still accept her.

She noticed Skylar, the small blond boy from her morning classes, sitting with a group of kids, although he was one seat away, at the end of the table, and no one seemed to be talking to him. A few tables over, the girl with the headscarf from social studies was sitting with two other girls. Lily froze when she saw Ryan stroll over to them. *Oh no, please no*, Lily thought.

Just as Ryan was passing Skylar, he noticed something and grabbed Skylar's lunch bag, shaking it out, though it was already empty. "One dumb sandwich again? Loser. And, dude, this is the same lunch bag!" In a mocking voice, he read the words on the bag. "'Wakanda Forever.' What are you, in kindergarten?" He smirked and dropped the bag on the floor, sauntering off as Skylar bent down to retrieve the bag.

Lily felt her eyes narrowing. Maybe Skylar only wanted one sandwich. Or maybe his family couldn't afford much food. Why would you make fun of someone for that? How did that make him a "loser"? And what was wrong with reusing a lunch bag? Or writing whatever you wanted on it?

Ryan was looking around for his next victim, so Lily sat abruptly at the end of a table and opened her book. She wasn't fast enough.

"Oh, look," Ryan's voice came from behind her, "it's the . . . *really smart* girl." He said it in a high-pitched way, making fun of Hobart's voice.

Lily tried hard to pretend she was engrossed in *Amal Unbound* although she knew her face was turning pink. She could feel the warmth rising in her cheeks. She startled when Ryan put his elbows on the table and leaned in toward her, his face close to hers. Lily backed away, letting go of her book and clutching her charm bracelet instead.

"Let me help you out here," Ryan said in a voice that was maybe meant to sound nice but sounded threatening. "You don't want to be friends with Ho-fart." The boys who were clustered around Ryan snickered. Ryan's face morphed into some semblance of a smile that looked more like a sneer.

It's Ho-BART, Lily wanted to say, but she didn't have the nerve.

"He's a loser and anyone who hangs with him is a loser. Understand?" Ryan's fake smile was now gone. He was staring at her, waiting for an answer. She couldn't move farther away from him because his buddies were standing on the other side of her, watching.

She knew what Ryan meant by "loser"—someone who'd be the target of bullying, just like Hobart.

"I said, do you understand?"

Lily gave a nod, hoping that would make him go away.

Ryan sneered. "You think you're smart because you're reading a book? You don't know what smart is."

"Hi, Lily!"

She recognized Hobart's voice and felt relieved, although guilty for feeling relieved.

"Hey, Ho-fart," Ryan said, "it's your *really smart* girl-friend, the mute."

Suddenly, Ryan noticed something at the other end of the cafeteria and moved away. Lily looked in the same direction and saw a large man in a bright blue sweatshirt walk briskly into the room.

"Are you okay?" Hobart asked, sitting next to her. "What did Ryan say?"

"He was supposedly welcoming me to school."

"Oh. I wouldn't trust him if I were you."

"I know that!" Lily snapped. She took a deep breath. "I'm sorry. I didn't mean to say it that way. I just feel . . . icky . . . after being around him. I'm still shaking."

"It's okay," Hobart said, "I get that way, too."

"Really?" Lily stared at him. "You look so calm."

"But my underarms are spraying like fountains! The sweat comes pouring out, and I mean, really pouring, like—"

"Okay, I get it, Hobart," Lily said, but couldn't help smiling.

Hobart smiled, too. "Do you like peanut butter cookies?"

Lily nodded. "My favorite."

Hobart put three large cookies on her tray. "You can have those. They're homemade."

"Don't you like them?"

"Yup!" Hobart pulled three more out of his lunch bag and grinned. "My mom loves baking! She also thinks I don't eat enough so she gives me *lots*."

"Remember what I said," Ryan's voice said over her shoulder, and she shuddered. He grabbed the cookies off of her tray before Lily could react.

"Why don't you put those back?" a deep, gravelly voice said from behind her.

Lily turned to see the man in the blue sweatshirt. She also noticed Hobart break into a grin.

"Oh, hello, Mr. Hammer," Ryan said, sounding polite. "She was giving them to me out of kindness."

Mr. Hammer's voice remained low and calm. "No, you were taking them from her out of meanness."

Hobart snorted and quickly slapped his hand over his mouth, though his eyes were still grinning.

Ryan dropped the cookies back on Lily's tray and walked away quickly.

"Yes!" Hobart said. "The Hammer is *in* the *house*! Lily, this is Mr. Hammer. He's a cafeteria monitor, which is a perfect job for him because he's an ex-cop!"

Mr. Hammer smiled and held out his palm to shake Lily's hand. "Any friend of Hobart's is a friend of mine."

Lily was momentarily frozen. That was exactly what her dad used to say about her friends, even though Lily didn't have many friends. Her dad said it to her stuffed animals when she was little, to real animals she befriended, and to the occasional kid Lily played with.

Mr. Hammer's manner was like her dad's, too, although in appearance they were complete opposites. Her dad was small and thin and not that old. Mr. Hammer looked like a grandfather and had the build of a football player. Her dad was pale and wore glasses. Mr. Hammer was African American and seemed to have particularly good eyesight, since at that moment, he called out to a boy standing several tables away—"Shawn, my man! You don't want to do that"—and the boy quickly lowered his hand that held a green apple and sat down.

"See?" Hobart said with a grin.

She did. On the inside, Mr. Hammer was very much like her dad, who would break up fights and stand up for anyone who was being treated badly.

"Can you believe he volunteers to do this? My mom says that makes him a saint. And isn't it cool his name is Hammer? He lets me call him *the* Hammer, like in curling."

"Curling?" Lily said as she watched Mr. Hammer approach a group of girls who were yelling at each other.

"My favorite sport! The hammer is powerful because it's the last stone shot. You can use it to knock out the other team's stones or make sure the hammer lands on the button, or at least somewhere in the house close to the button, and then your team gets the point—"

Hobart went on and on as Lily tried to listen, but the noise and smells of the cafeteria were overwhelming.

It was a different world from the kitchen island at their previous house where she and Dad used to eat lunch between homeschool lessons. Quiet. Calm. Just Dad doing silly stuff like making a topographical map with hummus mountains and lettuce oceans, and saying, "Cloudy with a chance of tomatoes!" as he dropped cherry tomatoes on top.

She'd barely managed a few bites of her salad when chimes sounded the end of lunch.

"Aw, man," Hobart said, "we need longer lunch periods!"

Lily agreed, but only if the Hammer was there.

Libro

I am insulted! How dare Ryan make fun of a book? In any form. Keep reading, Lily!

I'd like to send some choice words out to that sneeze-lurker right now.

Yes, I know I should not be a name-caller.

Deal with it.

You do know what a sneeze-lurker is, I assume? I should not assume. It is a person who throws pepper or snuff in someone's face in order to rob them. True, Ryan may not be robbing them of anything physical but, I ask you, is he robbing them of something intangible?

Hint: The answer is yes.

And, Mr. Sneeze-lurker, as for whether a book can help someone "deal" with the likes of you, or "deal" with anything for that matter, I CAN, INDEED.

Just read me.

Go ahead.

Read. My. Words.

That would really make my day.

Chapter 4

*L*ily lay on her bed, her chin resting on her arm, exhausted after her first day. All she wanted was to be homeschooled again. Skippy, their Labradoodle, sat with his chin on her bed, occasionally nudging her arm with his cold, wet nose.

"Wait, Skippy, I'm reading first, then we can play."

She opened the original letter from Dad. She must've read it a hundred times now. No, probably a thousand. She turned to the section about Strive for Five.

Be fair with yourself, Lily. Remember those sticker charts we made when you were little? And how hard you were on yourself? Like when you mispronounced "manure" in Charlotte's Web and

*refused to give yourself a sticker for reading it—
even though you were only six years old? If you
speak up or step out of your comfort zone, add a
charm to your bracelet, okay? Your first try can
be something very small. Just take that first step,
and each one will become easier.*

She put the letter down and opened the silver box with
five charms inside, each in its own section. She would earn
one every time she spoke up or stepped out. First was the
state charm, then one of the United States, then North
America, then a silver globe of the Earth, and finally, a
swirly blue, purple, and gold ball depicting the universe.

When Dad asked her to promise him that she would
Strive for Five, she had.

The next day he died.

Lily heard whining and felt the cold nose again.

"I'm sorry, Skippy, I just don't feel like playing."

Lily scratched behind Skippy's ears, but he shook his
head and promptly dropped a tennis ball next to her bed.

She sighed.

Skippy picked up the ball and laid it carefully on the bed
next to her, then stepped back and wagged his tail.

When she didn't throw the ball, he used his nose to push
it into her hand. And when that didn't work, he whined and
stared at her, his wrinkled eyebrows making him look so

concerned, Lily had to smile, which made him lick her face and wag his tail. And bark.

"Okay, okay," Lily said, pouring herself off of her bed. "I'll throw your ball."

One nice thing about moving to this tiny house was that it had a large fenced yard, perfect for Skippy. Since it was just Lily and her mom now, they only needed two bedrooms, one bathroom, a living room, and a kitchen. *Who uses a dining room, anyway?* her mom had said. And a small house was much quicker and easier to clean.

As she threw the ball for Skippy, Lily thought about the real reason they moved across town to a much smaller house. Dad's experimental cancer treatments cost way more than the insurance company would pay, and even though Mom was a lawyer and taught at the university, she still didn't make enough money to cover the bills. They had to sell their house. Lily didn't mind that. She would happily live in a cardboard box if money could've cured her dad. But it didn't. And the only thing she resented about this house was that it didn't have any memories of him. Even if some of the memories were sad.

Skippy dropped the ball at her feet, panting. She picked it up and threw it again. It reminded her of practicing for the geography bee with Dad. He would say the name of a country as he threw the ball for Skippy, and she had to tell him as much as she could about it—its capital, ethnic groups, economy—by the time Skippy returned with the ball, which wasn't very long, so she had to think fast.

In their old house, Dad had used seven rooms, including the dining room, the spare bedroom, his office, and the basement—none of which they had in this house—to represent the continents.

Africa was the kitchen because they needed all the cabinets and drawers, and every shelf and divider, to cover each of Africa's fifty-four countries. She still pictured what Dad called *"T*iny spoons" in the utensil holder when she thought of *T*ogo, and its capital, which also had an *o* like in *spoon*: Lomé. Immediately to the right were the *"B*ig spoons," that stood for *B*enin, east of Togo, and its capital with lots of *o*'s: Porto Novo.

Skippy's barking jerked her out of her memories.

"What?" Lily said. "I'm throwing it."

Skippy ran to the gate and Lily saw that her mom had parked along the curb in front of their house.

"Hi, sweetie!" Mom said, waving with one hand and pulling her briefcase from the back seat with her other. She was wearing the lilac suit Lily loved with the bright fuchsia blouse. Lily smiled as Mom did her usual getting home ritual of pulling the elastic from her ponytail, shaking her head, and letting her long, dark hair fall around her shoulders.

Skippy barked at the gate as Mom tried to open it. "Ugh! We've got to fix this latch!"

Lily tugged on the gate, which eventually opened.

Mom gave her a hug. "Come on, I want to hear all about your first day."

Lily sat at the kitchen table while Mom chopped sweet potatoes for roasting, Lily's favorite, and Skippy wedged himself between Mom and the counter, hoping some food would drop.

"I knew I wouldn't like school," Lily said softly, even though she felt like screaming it.

"Going to a neighborhood school is a good idea, though," Mom said. "You'll get to make friends with people who live close by. You'll be with kids all day." Mom hesitated for a moment before adding softly, "You know that's something your dad and I always disagreed on."

"Yeah, I know," Lily said. She knew that very well. It was the one thing Mom and Dad actually argued about. Dad had been bullied in school and was adamant about homeschooling Lily because she had the same shy, sensitive nature. Mom argued that Lily shouldn't be kept shielded and isolated. Dad always said that Mom didn't understand because she was a different kind of person.

Fortunately, Dad had always won.

Lily agreed with Dad. She wasn't isolated at all. She spent all day with Dad and often with other homeschooled kids. They went to hands-on educational events at museums where she had to work in groups, so it wasn't like she was never with other kids. She just wasn't in a classroom with the same kids or in a huge school, which was perfectly fine with Lily. Not being in regular school meant she could do things during the day, like volunteer at the food bank and thrift store, and even teach little kids English while Dad tutored their mothers. She would read to them in the play area of the library while their mothers took English lessons from Dad. It was perfectly fine. No, it was *perfect*.

"Skippy!" Mom said. "Will you stop getting in my way? I'm not giving you people food. It's not good for you. Lily, let him out, please."

Lily opened the kitchen door and took one of the balls from the basket on the stoop. "Here, Skip!" she said, distracting him from the kitchen counter. As Dad always said, Skippy never met a ball that wasn't his best friend, so he happily ran after it.

"I don't see why I can't be homeschooled," Lily grumbled, sitting back down at the table.

"It worked because your dad could meet his deadlines by writing in the evenings and on weekends. It wouldn't work with my schedule. Besides"—she gave Lily her wry smile—"would you really want me homeschooling you?"

Lily smiled back. She had a point. Lily loved her mother, but she wasn't a natural-born teacher for kids like Dad was. She got exasperated when Dad rearranged the house for a lesson. Mom's response was always, "Why does it have to be a game? Can't she just memorize it?"

Mom shook her head. "No, it's better for you to learn how to deal with your peers."

"The kids are rude and disrespectful, and my homeroom is loud and messy."

"Well," Mom said, tossing the sweet potatoes in olive oil, "you have to understand that you're a quiet, tidy, mature kid, so anyone is going to look loud and messy compared to you."

"And there are bullies."

Mom froze with the pan halfway into the oven. "What do you mean?" Lily knew Mom felt the same way as she did, and as Dad had, about bullies. Everyone should be treated fairly and with respect. "Were you bullied, honey?"

"Yes, they were making fun of me for reading a book."

Mom shut the oven door and turned to Lily. "What happened?"

Lily shrugged. "Nothing. This boy came over and they picked on him instead."

Mom frowned.

A piercing scream came from the yard. "Ahhh! It's a dog! A *dog*!"

Lily ran to the door and, before even opening it, saw Hobart through its window. He was on the ground. With Skippy on top of him. She turned to her mom. "That's the boy!"

Libro

Has that ever happened to you? Being teased or bullied? It has happened to most people. Where do you think the Imaginer got the idea? Oh, I'm not saying she has no imagination—she is the Imaginer, after all, and imagining is her greatest (perhaps her only) skill—but sometimes when you've been through something yourself, you're even better at imagining and describing it. I would say she had the experience herself, given the hard swallows and occasional nose blowing when she was writing those scenes. Or perhaps she's simply angry with Ryan, that sneeze-lurker. I know I am!

All right, all right, I suppose we should get back to poor Hobart where we left him. On the ground.

Chapter 5

"Skippy! Off!" Lily's mother yelled.

Lily ran over and grabbed Skippy's collar, pulling him away. "I'm sorry, Hobart! Are you okay?"

"Yes! I'm totally okay. I love dogs! AND YOU HAVE A DOG! Why didn't you tell me?"

"I just met you."

"Yeah, but a DOG! That's big! I've always wanted a dog! You're so lucky! My dad's allergic, so we can't have one."

Skippy picked up a tennis ball and headbutted Hobart's leg.

"Mom, this is Hobart," Lily said.

"Nice to meet you, Hobart."

"Can I throw balls for him? Please, please, please? Oh, and hi-nice-to-meet-you-too."

"Of course," Lily's mom said with a smile.

Lily smiled, too, as she watched Hobart and Skippy. They were both so exuberant.

"Hey!" said Hobart. "I get why he's called Skippy! When he runs it looks like he's skipping!"

Lily and her mom shared a look.

"That's exactly what Dad said, remember? And that's why he named him Skippy."

Lily's mom nodded. "I do remember."

Lily thought about how her dad, like Hobart's, was allergic to dogs, except that Dad had said, *Every kid needs a dog*. That's why they got a Labradoodle.

After a while, Skippy's tongue was hanging out and he was panting loudly. Mom said it was time to give him a rest.

"Oh! I almost forgot!" Hobart picked up a small red plaque from the grass and handed it to them. It said Love Makes a House a Home and had red glitter on it. "It's a housewarming gift from my mom."

"That's lovely," Mom said, brushing glitter off her skirt. "Thank you. Did she make it?"

"Nope! It's from the Dollar Store. You can get some really cool stuff there. I hope the sign helps. My mom says that after a stressful, life-altering event, you're not supposed to make any major changes. Like moving."

Lily's mom gave a tight smile. "Yes, well, thank you for that information, Hobart."

"You're welcome, even though it's a little late now. But

you know what? I'm really glad you moved into our neighborhood; otherwise, I wouldn't have a friend."

Mom tilted her head and her forehead wrinkled, but when she saw Hobart's big grin, her face relaxed. "I'm glad Lily has a friend, too."

"Hey, Lily! We can walk to school together. I'm just two blocks over. I can pick you up in the morning. I looked for you after school today, but you were gone."

"Oh . . . sorry." Lily had dashed out of the building and ran almost the entire way home to get away from school as quickly as possible.

"Maybe you two would like to walk Skippy together after school?"

Hobart looked like he'd won the lottery as he pumped his fist. "Yes! In the house!"

"Actually, outside would be better," Mom said.

"I know. 'In the house' is a curling term."

"Curling?" Mom said, her eyes looking up and to the left, the way they did when she was trying to remember someone's name or what she wanted to buy at the grocery store. "Is that where you slide those heavy disks to the other end of the ice?"

"Yup! 'In the house' means when you get your stone in the circle."

"Do you play a lot of curling?" Lily asked.

"Actually, it's 'Do you curl,' but no, there's no place around here. It's still my favorite sport. It takes a good eye and a lot of control to shoot a huge stone to the other end of the ice and make it stop exactly where you want. Really."

Lily wondered why Hobart seemed so anxious to convince them.

Mom's watch dinged. "Ah. The potatoes are ready. It's almost time for our dinner, Hobart."

"Oh! You guys are invited to dinner at our house on Saturday. Six p.m. sharp because Dad wants to watch the hockey game at eight. It gets really loud, then, and I mean LOUD!"

"You're hockey fans, too?" Mom said.

"Dad is. I only like curling. It's almost the same because it's on ice, it's just slower. And you don't have to wear skates. And you use brooms instead of hockey sticks. It's not an old man's sport, though." Hobart's face had lost any semblance of a smile. "And it's not for wimps."

Lily saw her mom narrow her eyes and press her lips together, and realized she was doing the same thing. "Of course it's not for wimps, Hobart. It sounds like a very interesting and challenging sport. We look forward to hearing more about it at dinner on Saturday."

As Hobart walked down the sidewalk, Skippy peered through the gate after him, craning his neck to the left to watch. Lily had to call Skippy several times before, with a frustrated whine, he finally turned away from the gate and came inside.

Libro

I don't like the sound of Hobart's father already. And I would prefer not to go to dinner at his house, but I have a feeling I'm going to be dragged there, anyway.

Sigh.

It's times like these I really wish I had some control over my own fate.

For one thing, the man is wrong about curling. I'm reading a book about it—yes, I'm a book; I read other books. Books are my friends. This should not be a surprise.

Curling is quite an interesting sport, actually. And infinitely more challenging than hockey, which, granted, is fast-paced and exciting, if bloody. Curling has the finesse of chess, the mental gymnastics of geometry and statistics, the relatively mild exercise of shooting stones, the more

aerobic exercise of vigorous sweeping, and the joy of officially sanctioned shouting. There are few injuries and even
fewer fights (if any). And one does not even need to learn
how to skate to be allowed on the ice. And no padding or
helmets. That is quite a number of desirable traits in one
sport.

I hope someone is able to enlighten Hobart's father. I
will pass, however. I don't even want to be in the same
room as that man. . . . Oh, that's right, we're having dinner.

Sigh.

Chapter 6

*L*ily tried hard to get used to school. By Thursday, she knew her schedule and could find her way around the building, but she still didn't like it. Especially homeroom. If anything, it was louder and more chaotic than the first day, except for the Pledge of Allegiance, when everyone, even Ryan, was quietly respectful.

People dumped their backpacks and lunch boxes any-where. There were scraps of paper—and books!—randomly spread out on the floor. There was even a rotting banana on the windowsill. Lily gripped her desk to anchor herself.

"I hope you're all talking about student council!" Miss Chase's voice was barely audible over the din. "The elec-tions are coming up. If you're interested, remember to sign up on the sheet in the cafeteria by the door. . . ."

Miss Chase's voice was drowned out by the chatter. Lily wondered if anyone was talking about student council. Ava and Samantha were definitely talking about fashion. Skylar looked like he was doing worksheets. With a calculator. Other kids were engrossed in their phones. Hobart was standing at his desk reading a book about curling, occasionally laughing out loud. Lily wished she could block out the noise so easily and read one of her own books she'd pulled from her backpack, *Amina's Voice*.

She watched Ryan go to the corner of the whiteboard by the door and make a fourth vertical line with a blue marker, smirking as he walked back to his buddies. He high-fived the boy who always wore a plaid shirt over a black T-shirt. The two boys kept whispering and looking over at Skylar, snickering. Lily figured the tally had something to do with Skylar. She also figured that whatever it was, it was mean.

"Two more minutes to talk about student council elections!" Miss Chase called out.

Hobart closed his book, sat down, and leaned over to Lily's desk. "Do you want to talk about the elections?"

Lily startled, staring at him.

"What's wrong?"

"Nothing. It's just . . . that's what my dad used to say. He was a political reporter."

"Really? Cool!" Hobart paused. "What does that mean, exactly?"

"He talked with people who were running for office, like school board or city council, about why they were interested and what they'd do if they got elected."

"Oh, that's what a reporter does? I thought they just wrote about what already happened."

"They do, but a good reporter finds out *why* things happen. The *why* is the heart of the story. That's what my dad said, anyway."

Hobart nodded slowly. "I like that. The *why*."

Lily felt a slight pain in the back of her throat as she twirled her charm bracelet around her wrist. "I always told him politics was boring."

"But talking to people about what they think isn't boring."

Lily nodded, wishing she'd seen what Hobart already saw. "My dad said politics, especially local government, impacts your day-to-day life, so it's important."

Hobart sat straight up. "Maybe you want to run for student council!"

Lily quickly shook her head. That was the last thing she would ever want.

"But local government is important."

"Do you want to run?" Lily asked him.

Hobart's shoulders fell. "Nah, I don't think anyone would vote for me."

"I would."

Hobart grinned, and the chimes sounded for math class.

In social studies, Lily was grouped with Ava and Samantha. She was still thinking about Dad, so it took her a while to key into their conversation, though it didn't seem related to immigration, which they were still studying.

"It's definitely the same pair of jeans," Samantha said, "because it has the same spots on the knee. Skylar's worn them four days in a row!"

"Without washing them?" said Ava. "Ew!"

Lily thought back to the blue lines on the whiteboard. So that was what Ryan's tally was about.

"Or," Ava said slowly, "it could be a stain. They might be clean."

"Then buy a new pair, duh!"

Ava nodded solemnly. "I know, right? They probably cost, like, five dollars at Walmart."

Maybe, Lily wanted to say, Skylar's family would rather spend five dollars on food or rent or bus money or a doctor's appointment or—

Samantha flipped her long blond hair. "You know what my sister and her friends do when they're bored? They drive to Walmart—"

"Samantha! Your sister shops at Walmart?" Ava's eyes were large.

"No! They go to Walmart and leave five-dollar bills on shelves in the store. For the poor people. They don't even do it for fame. They do it just to be nice!"

"That is so cool!"

"I know! She tried to use that for her high school community service requirement, but can you believe her teacher said that wasn't good enough?"

"That's outrageous!" Ava agreed. "What could be nicer than that?"

Samantha shrugged, shaking her head. "I don't know." When she glanced at Lily, her expression turned sour. "What?"

Lily realized that her face must've been showing her feelings. "Um . . . isn't community service usually, like, helping at a homeless shelter or a food pantry?"

Samantha tilted her head coyly. "Um," she said, "everyone does that. This was an original idea to help poor people."

Lily gave a nod simply to end the conversation. Didn't Samantha realize that going to Walmart didn't mean you were "poor"? And that finding five dollars would not exactly make someone rich? If they even kept it. Maybe they'd spend time asking people around them if they'd dropped any money. It wasn't really a "service" to toss money around when you had plenty and you were just bored.

The whole conversation made Lily feel a little sick. It wasn't that she felt embarrassed for being "poor." Lily didn't feel poor, though they did live, as Mom said, on a shoestring, which meant, for one thing, she didn't have extra five-dollar bills to leave on store shelves. It was more Samantha's attitude that leaving excess money in a store meant they were performing an amazing service—and they should be praised for it.

Lily was relieved when class was over. It was one of the "block" days to get them ready for middle school, so she had English before lunch. Fortunately, Hobart was in her class, which meant they had "B" lunch together.

Lily enjoyed English class. It was so much easier to write ideas than to speak them out loud. That way the reader could be in a completely different room and not be looking at you while they took in your words. Like Dad had said, *My voice is through my pen.*

She loved the books Mrs. Sanchez was having them read. Some of them she'd read, like *The Parker Inheritance*, *El Deafo*, and *Merci Suárez Changes Gears*, but she was looking forward to reading and doing an assignment on *Under the Mesquite*. The variety of activities they could do to report on a book—a trailer, a newspaper article, a play (which Lily would never do)—were the kinds of things Dad came up with. Mrs. Sanchez even said Hobart could rewrite a story and set it in a curling stadium with all the characters as team members.

At the end of class, as she and Hobart were leaving for

lunch, Mrs. Sanchez said, "Lily, can I talk to you for a minute?"

"I'll see you in the cafeteria," Hobart said. "I have to stop at my locker."

Mrs. Sanchez picked up a stack of books, turning the bindings so Lily could read the titles. "Lily, some of these books include the loss of a family member. Sometimes it can be healing to read about, but in case you're not ready for that yet, I can help you select others."

Lily gave a half shrug. "It's okay." She took one of her favorite books out of her backpack and showed it to Mrs. Sanchez.

"*The Bridge Home*? I love that one! There's sadness but it's so hopeful at the same time. Doesn't it feel real?"

"Yes," Lily said, without adding, *even the part about the bullies.*

When she arrived in the cafeteria, she saw Ryan holding Hobart's curling book and laughing. He kept raising the book above his head as Hobart jumped wildly, shouting, "Give it back!" She wished Hobart would stop jumping so Ryan's friends would stop laughing at him. She wished she could do something. Mostly, she wished Ryan would just give Hobart's book back.

Suddenly, the book was snatched from Ryan's hand.

"I'll take that," Mr. Hammer said.

Lily hadn't even seen him, but now her heart could stop

racing. She slumped down at their table as Ryan and his friends scurried away.

"Wow!" Hobart said with a grin. "It's not even your regular day—you don't work Tuesdays and Thursdays!"

"I switched because we're flying to Florida tonight to visit our new grandbaby."

Hobart was still basking in the glow of having been saved. "You're like a knight in shining armor!"

"Or one in khaki pants," Mr. Hammer said with a wink.

"Or, I know," Hobart said, "Black Panther!"

Mr. Hammer looked over to the next table at Skylar, pumped his fist in the air, and said, "Wakanda forever!"

Skylar gave a small smile and held up his worn lunch bag that said, Wakanda Forever!

Mr. Hammer pointed at him. "I *like* you, Skylar!"

For the first time, Lily saw Skylar grin.

Hobart was paging through his curling book, *Bare Bones Stones*, showing it to Mr. Hammer.

"Hold on," Mr. Hammer said, taking the book and flipping back a few pages to read a sticky note. "What on earth is a 'Manitoba tuck'?"

"It's a way of shooting the stone. I'll demonstrate!" Hobart crouched way down on his left foot, pushing his right leg straight out behind him. His chin was practically on the floor. "See?"

Lily was glad the Hammer was there, or Ryan would

definitely make fun of Hobart lying on the cafeteria floor. He and his gang were already laughing at him as it was.

Hobart popped back up and sat at the table. "It's the way some people on the Manitoba teams send their stone down the ice. Most people don't go down so far. When I'm on a curling team, I'm totally doing that move." Hobart stole a look over at Ryan's table, where the boys were still laughing, and his shoulders drooped.

"Never mind them," Mr. Hammer said. "They can't do a Manitoba tuck."

Lily swallowed and made herself speak up. "They don't even know what a Manitoba tuck *is*."

"Exactly!" the Hammer said. "They are completely Manitoba tuck-less!"

That made them all laugh.

As shouting erupted in the far corner of the cafeteria, Mr. Hammer sighed. "Lily, do you know exactly how this curling game works?"

Lily shook her head.

"Hobart, you need to explain it to her, so she can explain it to me. My only sport is fantasy football." He gave them a wink and headed over to the commotion.

A balled-up piece of paper landed on the table near Hobart. "Oh, great," Hobart said, opening it and reading it, then crushing it back into an even smaller ball.

"What does it say?" Lily asked, although hearing the

laughter from Ryan's table, she guessed it wasn't good.

"Just that I'm a dork."

Lily looked over at Ryan, who was high-fiving one of his guffawing friends. The boy in the black T-shirt and plaid shirt, however, seemed like he was only forcing a grin while he cracked his knuckles repeatedly.

"Who's the boy in the plaid shirt?"

Hobart sighed. "Brady. We were best friends in third grade."

"Really? What happened?"

"He started hanging out with Ryan more and more in fourth grade. And by last year he was part of the gang."

"Why?"

Hobart shrugged. "His parents got divorced and my mom said he was acting out to get his dad's attention. His dad was really cool—before the divorce, I mean. He used to shoot off rockets in their backyard or take us fishing or go-kart racing, all kinds of stuff. I think it was because Brady's the only boy. He's got three older sisters and, trust me, they're all annoying." He frowned. "I guess he needed a bunch of guys . . . just . . . not including me." Hobart's usual smiling face was glum.

"Oh." Lily wished she hadn't brought up a sad subject. "Can you tell me about curling?"

"Well, basically, you've got this long narrow ice rink and at either end there's a big red circle with a small blue circle inside, which is called the house—are you sure you've never seen curling?"

"Positive." Lily could see that Hobart was beginning to feel lighter, so she added, "I'd like to learn, though. Also, I need to explain it to Mr. Hammer, like he said."

"Okay. The goal is to stand at one end and push this circular weight—it's called a stone and it has a flat bottom and a handle on top—to the other end and get it in the house, as close to the center, called the button, as you can. Whoever's stone is closest to the center wins!"

"It sounds kind of like horseshoes," Lily said.

Hobart thought for a moment. "I guess, but horseshoes doesn't use brooms."

"What are the brooms for?"

"After one person delivers the stone—that means shooting it—one or two teammates sweep really fast in front of the stone because that makes the ice heat up, which reduces friction, which makes the stone go straighter. It's really cool! Do you want to see it sometime?"

"Sure."

"Deal! I've got a whole curling DVD. Just let me know when you want to watch it!"

Chimes, met with a collective groan, signaled the end of lunch. As Lily and Hobart stood up, Lily saw Ryan laughing at the sign by the door with big red letters: Student Council Candidate Sign-up Sheet. He gave the sign a slap.

"Let's hope he doesn't sign up," Hobart said.

"How much power does a student council have?" Lily said.

"Well, maybe not that much."

Lily gave a half shrug.

"But, like your dad said, it's local government. It's still important."

Lily watched Ryan's gang follow him out of the cafeteria, with Brady, head down, trudging after them at the tail end of the group.

Libro

I don't know what they'd do without the Hammer. Wouldn't it be brilliant if everyone had a Mr. Hammer to help them with sneeze-lurkers like Ryan, who are always stirring up trouble?

Speaking of bullies, and their cohorts, like Brady . . . there are many things you can say about a bully, and most of them are probably true, but it's also true that a bad guy or a bad situation is a test—or let's call it an opportunity—to show what you're made of. Are you up for the challenge? I suspect you are.

If you're a bully reading this, by the way, your test is dealing with the bully, too—you. The good news is, you can turn things around. Be prepared for people not to believe you at first because you've been acting like a sneeze-lurker for a long time. You'll have to show your non-sneeze-lurker-tude for a while before people will trust you. Are *you* up for the challenge? I suspect you are.

Chapter 7

On their walk home, Hobart taught Lily more about curling. "Do you know what a flash is?"

Lily shook her head. "No."

"It's when your stone misses every other stone in the house!"

"And the house is at the end of the ice," Lily confirmed.

"Right, the bull's-eye at the end of the ice, except the ice is called the sheet. Now, for curling statistics: there's shooting percentage, sweep percentage, and degree of difficulty. . . ."

Lily tried to take it all in, but Hobart spoke so quickly it was hard to keep all the statistics straight. Still, it made her smile to see his enthusiasm.

When they reached Lily's house, Hobart stopped to

read the sign in the front yard. *No matter where you are from, we're glad you're our neighbor.*

"Where did that come from?"

"My mom must have put it up before she left for work."

Hobart nodded but didn't say anything.

"The other languages are Spanish and Arabic, but they say the same thing," Lily explained.

"Uh-huh," Hobart said.

"I think we need one at school," Lily added.

"Yeah," Hobart said without enthusiasm. "How come?"

Lily realized that Hobart wasn't in her social studies class, and she didn't actually know how he felt about immigration. "We're talking about immigration in social studies, and the different countries students at our school came from. Um . . . you're okay with immigrants, right?"

"Definitely. And my mom, too."

Lily paused for a moment. "Oh." She realized that Hobart's dad was not.

Before she could ask about it, Skippy started barking from the kitchen, standing on his hind legs, scratching at the window of the door. When Lily let him out, he howled at them some more, as if telling them what he thought about being left alone all day.

Hobart laughed. "He sounds like a rooster crowing!"

Skippy ran in circles, then to a bush to relieve himself, then in more circles, then licked Lily's face and jumped on Hobart.

"Skippy, off!" Lily said.

"I don't mind," Hobart said.

"I know, but he has to learn not to jump because what if he knocks over a little kid?"

"Okay. Off, Skippy. See? I'll crouch down and pet you. You don't need to jump."

As they walked an excited Skippy to the nearby park, Hobart said, "I think that sign is cool. I just don't want my dad to drive past and see it."

"Why not?"

"It'll make him mad."

"Really? Why?"

Hobart wouldn't meet her gaze.

"Would he take it? Or destroy it?"

"No! Nothing like that. But he might decide I shouldn't be friends with you."

"What?" Lily was stunned. How could a grown-up act that way? And besides, the more she thought about it . . . "I think *you* get to decide who your friends are, Hobart."

He nodded slowly as if he hadn't considered the idea before. "Yeah, I guess so."

"We have a lot of refugees from Latin America, Iraq, and Afghanistan living in our neighborhood, so *people*"—and by *people* she meant Hobart's dad—"just have to get used to it. We should be really grateful to some of the men from Iraq and Afghanistan because they were translators and drivers for our military. Their lives were in danger every day."

"Wow," said Hobart. "Why would they even do that?"

"Because they wanted to make things better in their country."

"How come you know so much about this?" Hobart asked.

"My mom's an immigration lawyer. And my dad sometimes wrote about it because of the politicians he was covering. Plus, my mom asked him to tutor immigrants in English because he was an excellent instructor. Well, she didn't really ask, she basically told him. When my mom gets 'a bee in her bonnet,' as my dad said, you kind of have no choice. He really was a great teacher, though. He homeschooled me until . . . until now."

"Did you like being homeschooled?"

Lily nodded. "I loved it."

"How is it different?"

"In every way, like no noisy cafeteria. At lunchtime, and lots of times during the day, we had 'Skippy breaks,' when we played games with Skippy."

Skippy's ears perked up and he turned to look at her.

"What kind of games?"

"Hide-and-seek with his toys, piggy in the middle with his ball, tag—which he always won, of course."

"Oh, man, that would be so fun!" Hobart leaned over to

scratch Skippy's head. "I wish we could have Skippy breaks. Or any breaks. Homeschooling sounds awesome."

They walked in silence the rest of the way to the park. Lily thought about her dad, and how her mom started sort of homeschooling her in February, after Dad died. Mom worked at home for several months, and then only mornings until last week. It was what Mom referred to as their "recovery period" where they were "cocooning" and "dealing with our pain." Lily thought back on the past six months and it just felt like darkness.

At the dog park, Hobart threw a ball for Skippy until Skippy dropped it somewhere and couldn't find it; then he spent his time sniffing the fence, the trees, everywhere.

Hobart was fiddling with the latch on the gate of the dog area and staring at Lily.

"What?" Lily said, realizing she'd been thinking about her dad and hoping she hadn't missed something Hobart said.

"I just—" Hobart let go of the latch and stuffed his hands in his pockets. "I never said sorry about your dad, but I am. He sounds like he was a really good dad."

Lily nodded. "He was the best." When Hobart looked at the ground, she added quickly, "I mean, I guess everyone thinks their dad is the best."

"Yeah, I guess," Hobart said, not very convincingly. He took a deep breath and said quickly, "My dad had a friend who was killed in Afghanistan, so that's why he's against immigration."

"Oh. I'm sorry about his friend."

"Yeah. My mom says he's bitter. I call it angry."

"But," Lily said, "the people who want to be American citizens aren't the ones who killed your dad's friend."

"I know. But my dad says if you're patriotic, you wouldn't want any of those people here. It's disrespectful to soldiers."

Lily didn't think that was true. "My dad interviewed people who were running for office who'd fought in the Middle East. They got to know people in those countries and wanted them to be able to move here. That's why the IRC brings immigrants to live in our town."

"What's the IRC?"

"International Rescue Committee. My mom helps with that group. She says immigrants are really nice and caring, but people don't realize that because they don't take the time to get to know them."

Hobart looked at her for a moment, then looked away. "My mom says it's complicated."

"They always say that when it's something bad," Lily said. That's what her mom had told her when she announced they were moving, and that Lily would have to go to regular school.

"Or," Hobart said, "when they're making excuses."

Lily heard a choking sound and spun around to see

Skippy heaving. "Skippy! What's wrong?" She ran over to him, followed closely by Hobart.

"Oh my gosh, Skippy!" Lily looked at the empty cupcake and candy wrappers around her dog.

Just then, Skippy wretched a wad of wet cardboard.

"Is he okay?" Hobart asked.

Skippy picked up the ball he'd found and headbutted Hobart. He dropped the ball at Hobart's feel and backed away, wagging his tail and barking.

"I think he's fine," Lily said, "but people should be more careful and put their trash *in* the trash can instead of all around it."

"Yeah, and if you toss it and miss, then pick it up!" Hobart added as he snatched the cupcake and candy wrappers from the ground.

"Cupcakes, candy, even foods like peanut butter," Lily explained, "can have xylitol in them, which is really bad for dogs."

Skippy was still barking so Hobart threw the ball for him. "What happens to them?"

"Their insulin spikes, their blood sugar falls, their liver fails, and they die."

"That's *really* bad," Hobart said, giving Skippy a long head rub before throwing the ball again. "How do you know all this stuff, Lily?"

"My dad and I are . . . were . . . both dog lovers so we did a whole unit on dogs, including health and safety."

Hobart nodded. "Homeschooling sounds pretty cool."

"With my dad it was. I'm not sure it'd work so well with my mom. Sometimes one parent is better at something than the other."

"Yeah," Hobart said, "I know what you mean."

When it was time to go, Hobart wouldn't leave the park until they'd picked up every scrap of food and food wrapper they could find.

Libro

Oh, that is just peachy.[1]

Now I'm going to worry about Skippy and someone feeding him something he's not supposed to have.
How could you name a dog Skippy and not expect people to want to feed him peanut butter? Excuse me while I
research whether Skippy has xylitol. . . .

It does not.

However, fat is not good for dogs and can give them
pancreatitis. And the list goes on. And on.

Oh, my aching spine! This had better not be one of

---

1   Incidentally, peach pits are poisonous to dogs as well as humans.
I found that out while doing my research. This is why reading is
good. It can save your life. Literally.
    You're welcome.

those dead dog books. I have a soft spot for dogs. Like me, they have thoughts and feelings but no voice, or at least, they have difficulty in making themselves understood. I feel their frustration.

I will have to do some of my own editing-on-the-sly if the Imaginer dares kill off a dog. I am not having it. Not on my watch.

Chapter 8

By Friday, Miss Chase had actually progressed to writing math problems on the whiteboard and some people were even trying to listen—those who weren't on their phones. Skylar's desk was at the front of a row and he often answered Miss Chase's questions, along with Hobart and Zoey, the girl with spiked pink hair who sat next to Skylar. Skylar's voice was so low, it seemed that only Miss Chase could hear him. But she said, "That's right!" so often that Ryan started imitating her from the back of the room, which cracked up his gang.

Miss Chase was just about to erase Ryan's tally, now up to five marks, when she stopped. "Is this something important?"

The boys in the back giggled.

"Yeah," said Ryan.

"What's it for?" Miss Chase asked.

Other people in the class were snickering now. Lily felt her teeth clench and her eyes narrow.

"A project," Ryan said.

"Oh, cool!" Hobart said. "Like a statistics project?"

"Yeah," Ryan said as his cronies giggled, "a statistics project."

"Can I help? I've done a lot of statistics in curling!"

"Don't worry," Ryan said, trying not to laugh, "you can be part of the next one."

Lily cringed. What horrible, mean tally would they make for Hobart?

When she heard a boy whisper, "Bow tie," she knew. Hobart wore a bow tie every day. That's what they were going to make fun of.

She was upset through social studies, all the way until the end of class when Mrs. Barry said, "Listen up! No sixth graders are running for student council yet, so let's get educated about the process. What do you need to start with?"

Ideas, Lily thought. *A platform.* But she was too shy to raise her hand.

"Anyone?" Mrs. Barry said, her hands on her hips.

"A president?" someone asked softly. Lily turned and saw that it was the girl with a headscarf.

"Yes, Dunya. Impressive!" Mrs. Barry looked at the rest of the class. "Anyone else brave enough to answer?"

Lily wished she were but instead shrank down in her chair.

"Well," Mrs. Barry continued, "what do we need to know about the president, or any of the candidates?"

"If they're even from our school?" Ryan said.

Mrs. Barry sighed. "I think we can take that as a given. Any other thoughts?"

A platform, Lily thought again, willing someone to say it.

"A platform," Mrs. Barry finally said. "I'm sure you've heard that term."

"Like a stage?" Ryan said, trying to be funny.

"No, what they should say once they're *on* the stage." She folded her arms and looked at the class. "What are some things you'd like your student council to do for you?"

"PE all day!" a boy shouted.

"No!" a girl answered. "How about no PE?"

"I love PE!" another girl said. "How about Fridays off?"

"Lunch all day!"

"Ban school!"

"Let's keep it real, people," Mrs. Barry said. "What about some specific changes that are doable, like something in the cafeteria maybe?"

More monitors, Lily thought, *play music to make it a more pleasant experience, ban straws.*

"How about banning straws," Zoey, the math whiz from homeroom, said.

"Excellent!" said Mrs. Barry. "That's the idea. Now, think about a quick way to hook people. How would you do that?"

A slogan, Lily thought.

"Make a YouTube video," a boy said.

"Shorter," Mrs. Barry hinted.

"A short YouTube video?"

Slogan, Lily thought again.

"A party!" Ryan said. "That would get my attention!"

There was laughter and chatting about what to serve at a party as Mrs. Barry clapped her hands to quiet people down.

Finally, someone said *slogan* just before the chimes signaled end of class, and Mrs. Barry said, "Thank you! At least someone is paying attention."

Lily was crushed. She was paying attention. She was just too shy to speak. She thought of Dad again and his Strive for Five theory. If she spoke up five times, would it really be easier the sixth time?

As she entered the cafeteria, she passed Dunya, the girl with the headscarf from social studies. Lily hesitated, turned around, and quickly said, "Assalamu alaikum," an Arabic greeting. Dunya stared at her, stunned. Lily quickly turned and hurried to her table. Had she done something insulting? Had she pronounced it wrong? The women her dad taught said her accent was excellent, but maybe they were just being nice.

Embarrassed, Lily was happy to sit quietly and eat her lunch while Hobart talked about curling. A few minutes later, Lily noticed Dunya hurriedly getting up from her table as a teacher beckoned to her and some other kids with *English for Everyone* books. *Gosh*, Lily thought, *they have even less time for lunch than the rest of us.*

Dunya rushed past Lily's table and, with a smile, said, "Wa alaikum salam."

Lily smiled, too.

Hobart stared after her. "What did she say?"

"It's the answer to the greeting I said to her, *Peace be upon you*. It's Arabic."

"You know Arabic?"

"Just that greeting." Lily knew Dad would be proud of her. She had left her comfort zone, even though it didn't really count as "speaking up" because it was only to one person, and it wasn't exactly a conversation, just a greeting. Still, it was something.

As she walked down the hall at the end of the day, Lily saw Skylar, shoulders hunched, scurrying away from Ryan, who was calling "Loser!" after him. She felt her fists clench. How could he be so mean and get away with it?

Lily was passing homeroom, seething, when she noticed

Ryan's tally, still on the whiteboard. Taking a deep breath, she looked inside the room, saw it was empty, ran in, grabbed the eraser, and wiped out his marks.

As she ran out of the classroom, she noticed Brady from Ryan's gang, Hobart's former best friend. He gave her a funny look. She felt her face grow hot, but she didn't even care. She felt powerful. She hadn't used her voice exactly, but she'd taken a stand and that was something.

Libro

Oh. You're back.

My apologies. I was distracted by watching Lily.

Sometimes, even though I love words, I feel as if I'm watching a movie. A good book does that.

By the way, the book is almost always better than the movie. There are only three exceptions, but I won't share them because if I did, the Imaginer would delete them anyway, being highly biased toward books. Which I am, too, incidentally.

But back to Lily. Can you believe she erased Ryan's tally? Huzzah! Normally, I am not a fan of deletions, but sometimes, as they say, "less is more."

Brava, Lily!

Chapter 9

Saturday evening, Lily's mom yanked their stiff gate open, grumbling, "We have to fix this," as they headed to Hobart's house for dinner.

Lily held the large bouquet of flowers from the grocery store that Mom had insisted on buying. At least she'd listened to Lily about not bringing dessert since Hobart's mom liked baking so much.

As soon as they reached the Halls' front walk, Hobart yanked the door open and announced, "Lily and Mrs. Flippin are *in* the *house!*" which made them laugh.

Lily breathed in the aroma of fried something and she was instantly back at Sal's, Dad's favorite diner, eating fried chicken, mashed potatoes, and corn.

Mom handed Hobart's mom the flowers. "Thank you

so much for having us, Mrs. Hall. I hope you like peonies."

"Oh, please call me Nicole, and I love peonies!" She held the blossoms up to her nose and took in their fragrance. "Beautiful."

"She loves *all* flowers!" Hobart said with a grin.

"I'm Ron," Hobart's dad said, pushing between his wife and son. His bright hockey jersey contrasted with the pale green skirt and sweater set Mrs. Hall wore.

"I'm Laura," Mom said, "and this is my daughter, Lily."

Mr. Hall nodded at Mom, ignoring Lily. "Welcome to the neighborhood. Hobart says you used to live in River Oaks?"

"Hobart," Mrs. Hall said, "be a dear and put these in water, and then maybe you and Lily would like to pour us all some lemonade?"

Hobart grabbed the flowers. "Sure! Come on, Lily, the kitchen is this way."

"I know," Lily murmured, realizing that Hobart's house was laid out exactly the same as hers, only in reverse. It was a little disconcerting seeing all the rooms backward. The décor was different from her house, too. Where hers was simple and modern, Hobart's was old-fashioned and cozy, with flowered chairs that matched the frilly living room curtains, little glass dishes with candy, and signs with bows everywhere, like the Love Makes a House a Home sign Hobart had brought them.

Hobart put the flowers in a vase, which Lily brought to the dining room table as he lined up colorful striped glasses on the counter. When he opened the fridge, Lily noticed all the magnets with sayings, a National Wildlife calendar, and a pink notepad imprinted with "The Hall Family Shopping List." Above everything, though, was a photograph of a smiling young woman in fatigues, standing in a desert.

"Who is she?" Lily asked.

Hobart stopped pouring lemonade to look. "Oh! That's Melissa."

"Is she a relative?"

"No, she used to be my babysitter. Her mom and my mom are best friends. My mom calls herself Melissa's other mother." He put the lemonade bottle back in the fridge. "She's kind of like my big sister." He stared at the photo for a moment and his forehead wrinkled.

"Where is she?"

"Iraq," Hobart said quietly. "We email her, though. And my mom sends her cookies all the time." He continued looking at the photo. "She's got five and a half more months there."

Lily almost asked if he was worried about her, but realized she already knew the answer.

When they sat down to eat, Lily and her mom sat on one side of the table opposite Hobart, who gave them a huge smile.

"This is cool! You should come over a lot. I always wanted a bigger family."

"Hey, Tiny," Mr. Hall said, "pass those pork chops."

"Now, Ron," Hobart's mom said, "he's not even eleven yet. He'll grow."

Lily stared across the table at Hobart. "You're only ten?"

"See?" Mr. Hall said. "Still a little kid."

"I—I mean," Lily said, her face feeling hot, "you must be really smart to be in sixth grade."

"Nah," Hobart said, "my birthday's in December so they let me start a little early, that's all."

"And you're smart, too," Mrs. Hall said. "I knew you would be. That's why we named you Hobart." She looked at Lily. "It means 'shining intellect.'"

Hobart blushed and tried to hide a grin.

Mr. Hall laughed. "And you told me it was the capital of Tasmania, so I thought he'd be tough like the Tasmanian Devil. Instead of hockey, he likes curling. Curling! Can you believe it?"

Mrs. Hall gave him a frown, then turned to Lily's mom. "I love the name Lily. Is it a family name?"

Mom twirled her wedding ring around her finger. "Actually, it was the first flower my husband gave me. He didn't even know it was my favorite. It just seemed the perfect name for our daughter." Lily knew the family joke that was coming next. "Of course, he said we should've named her

81

La Paz, the capital of Bolivia, both for her peaceful nature and the fact that she loves geography, just like he . . ."

Mom looked down at her plate, blinking, and Lily's eyes felt hot as she remembered how the sentence always ended, "just like he . . . *does*." Except now it was . . . *did*.

After a pause, Mr. Hall cleared his throat. "How are you liking your new house?"

Mom forced a smile. "Oh, it's fine, but it's not in the best of shape."

"That's because renters lived there," Mr. Hall explained, "and they didn't take good care of it. I'm a licensed contractor, so if I can help out, let me know."

Lily saw Mom stiffen. "I'm trying to take care of things myself as much as possible—"

"I meant for free," Mr. Hall said. "That's what neighbors do for neighbors."

"Well, thank you. You know—" Lily knew Mom was about to mention the gate latch, but Mr. Hall kept talking.

"Of course, I hardly recognize my own neighborhood anymore."

Lily saw Hobart and his mom look at each other, their eyes wide. Mrs. Hall fiddled with the strands of glass beads she was wearing, which made a clacking sound.

Lily's mom smiled. "I know what you mean. My hometown has gotten so built up I hardly recognize it."

"I mean our whole society has changed," Mr. Hall said. "I can go into the hardware store and not hear a word of

English. I feel like a stranger in my own town!" He forced a laugh, but he wasn't smiling.

Mom's mouth fell open and stayed that way for a moment until she spoke. "I'm pretty sure they feel more like strangers than you, given that you've lived here your whole life."

"Exactly, I was born here. It's too easy for them to come in."

"Now, Ron, you know that's not how Melissa feels."

"She's too liberal," Mr. Hall grumbled, "so she can't see the truth."

Mrs. Hall frowned.

Hobart glanced at Lily and looked away.

Lily gripped the seat of her chair and prepared herself for what was to come.

Mom swallowed hard and put down her fork. "Actually, it's very difficult and takes a long time to become an American citizen. What's easy is being born here. I'm an immigration attorney and even if all goes smoothly, it takes years and very hard work to become a citizen."

Mr. Hall grunted. "That's not what I hear on the news."

Mom put on the tight smile Lily recognized. It meant the opposite of happy. "Sometimes I find that news shows are trying to scare us. That's how they get attention and increase their ratings. There's some false and misleading information out there, so I always try to find out what's really going on."

"You mean look for the *why*?" Hobart said.

Mom turned to stare at him, and her tight smile relaxed into a real one. "Exactly, Hobart."

Mr. Hall muttered something Lily couldn't make out, but he was clearly displeased.

There was a short, awkward silence until Mrs. Hall started talking nonstop about school and church and Pinterest and *The Great British Baking Show.* Finally, she said, "I think it's time for dessert!"

The lemon meringue pie Mrs. Hall made melted in Lily's mouth. She saw Mom close her eyes for a moment and let out an "Mmmm."

"Nicole is an amazing cook and even better with baking," Mr. Hall said.

"I'd like to start selling baked goods at the Saturday morning farmers' market in the parking lot of St. Paul's. Do you know about that?"

"No," Mom said, "but I'll definitely check it out."

"In the winter, they have the market inside the parish hall," Mrs. Hall continued.

"Yeah," Mr. Hall broke in, "but she's too embarrassed to drag her table and chairs and all her goods in my noisy truck that spews black smoke." He chuckled. "It still works, though!"

Mrs. Hall rolled her eyes.

"Don't worry," he told her. "The new pickups are in the showroom now so they're cutting prices on last year's models. Between that and trading in the old one we can swing it."

"Yes!" Hobart said.

"Will you help me at the market, Hobart?"

"Sure!"

Mr. Hall laughed. "Put a pointy hat on him and he can be your little elf!"

Suddenly, the dessert didn't taste so great anymore. Lily saw Mom purse her lips, then glance down at her watch. "Oh, look! The hockey game is starting soon."

"You're hockey fans?" Mr. Hall said.

"No, but I understand you are."

"Just me. Hobart here won't even watch it. He likes the old man sport of curling."

Hobart looked down at his plate.

"Actually," Mom said, "we're quite interested in curling, aren't we, Lily?"

Lily nodded. "I'm learning a lot already. I can practically do a Manitoba tuck."

Hobart flashed her a grin. "When do you want me to bring over my DVD?"

"Now, Hobart," his mother said, "you shouldn't invite yourself over."

Lily looked at her mom and raised her eyebrows. Mom smiled back. Lily knew they were thinking the same thing. Sundays were traditionally girls' night but lately, well, every night was girls' night.

"How about tomorrow night?" Lily said.

"In the house!"

As they walked home, Mom put her arm around Lily's shoulder and held her close. "I'm glad you invited Hobart over."

"Me, too."

"And I'm glad you're friends with him, honey. It must be tough getting teased at home and at school. I hope you'll look out for him."

On Sunday, Lily worked on her English homework, writing her report on *Under the Mesquite* in free verse, like the author had. Then she did her math problems and social studies questions for the week. They were easy. She and Dad had done all the work already. There was really no new material. She considered making the argument again to Mom that homeschooling was better than regular school, but she knew what the answer would be. Besides, if she were homeschooled, where would that leave Hobart?

As soon as Hobart walked in the door Sunday evening, Skippy barked and ran in circles, bringing Hobart one stuffed animal or ball after another until his toy basket was empty.

"I love this dog!" Hobart said as he threw toys randomly around the living room, down the hall, and into the kitchen, Skippy rushing back with each one, dropping it at his feet, wagging his tail and barking. Hobart even grabbed a stuffed hedgehog, squeaked it, then ran down the hall himself, with Skippy running and barking after him. Then Skippy came tearing into the living room with the hedgehog, Hobart chasing him.

Lily loved hearing her mother laugh as she watched Hobart and Skippy. She realized it had been a long time since she'd heard that.

When the doorbell rang, Skippy ran to the door, crowing his rooster bark.

"It's okay, Skippy," Lily said, holding him by the collar, as her mom paid the pizza delivery girl. Girls' night was always pizza night.

"We're having pizza?" Hobart's eyes were wide. "*In* the *house!*"

At the table, Skippy headbutted Hobart's knee.

"Lie down, Skippy!" Lily commanded. "Sorry, Hobart. He always tries that with a new person but he *knows*"—she looked down at Skippy—"that he's not supposed to beg at the table."

Hobart grinned at Skippy. "I don't mind."

"Well," Lily's mom said, "we can't let him get away with it or he'll do it all the time. That would get annoying."

Hobart looked down at Skippy, who was staring at him as if he were starving. While still lying down, Skippy managed to edge himself toward Hobart. He rolled over with his paws in the air like he was begging on his back.

"Skip-py," Lily said in a warning tone.

Skippy sighed, rolled over, and put his head on the floor.

"If I leave the table," Hobart said, "is it okay to give him a pizza crust?"

Mom shook her head. "It's better for dogs to never have people food."

Lily didn't totally agree. Some foods were bad, but Dad had always given Skippy people food, healthy things like carrots and sweet potatoes. Mostly. True, the pork fat and ice cream Dad gave him weren't the best choices, but Lily didn't believe that was why Skippy had gotten sick. Even then, the vet said to feed him boiled chicken and white rice. That was people food.

After dinner, they sat on the living room couch, Hobart in between Lily and her mom, explaining every action in the curling video. It could've been boring except that Hobart was so animated, even jumping up to demonstrate many of the moves, that it was actually fun. Lily's mother was laughing again.

"Show Mom the Manitoba tuck," Lily said.

Hobart crouched way down until he was almost flat on the floor. Skippy's ears perked up as he watched.

"That's impressive," Mom said. "And on ice, no less."

"Yup, someday I'm doing that in a real game. Once I find a curling place. And a team."

Skippy got up from his bed and stretched his legs out in front of him, chest on the floor, and his butt in the air.

Hobart grinned. "Not quite. You have to put your butt down for a Manitoba tuck!"

Skippy plopped his butt on the floor and quickly rolled over, legs in the air, looking at Hobart.

They all laughed, and Hobart said, "He just invented the Manitoba tuck-and-roll!"

Skippy wagged his tail, and Hobart scratched the dog's stomach until Skippy's eyes were starting to close and it looked like he was grinning.

Mom's phone rang and she pulled it out of her pocket to answer. "Okay, sure, I'll tell him." She put her phone back. "Hobart, your dad was at the hardware store so he's swinging by to pick you up."

Hobart's face fell. "I can walk."

Mom looked through the front window. "It's already dark. I'm afraid we got a little carried away."

"Okay, I'll go wait for him." Hobart leaped from the couch and grabbed his DVD.

"It'll be a few minutes," Mom said, but Hobart was already at the front door, opening it.

"That's okay, he . . . he likes me to be ready. Thanks for dinner. That was awesome."

Lily's mom stared at the now closed door. "Why don't you go wait with him."

As soon as Lily stepped onto the front porch, she realized the problem. Hobart was eyeing their yard sign, welcoming people in English, Spanish, and Arabic, and giving it a wide berth. He walked as far away from it as he could while still being near the Flippins' house.

Lily's shoulders sagged. Hobart shouldn't have to distance himself from a sign like that. He was probably relieved that it was almost dark so his dad might not be able to read the sign, even if he noticed it.

She had just walked up to Hobart when he pointed at headlights approaching. "That's my dad's truck. You can hear it a mile away. So," he said, looking everywhere but at her, "thanks for dinner, that really was awesome—pizza is my absolute favorite but we only order it on special occasions—and maybe I can come over again sometime, if that's okay, so, yeah, so I'll see you in the morning for school, okay, bye."

Lily waved at Hobart as he climbed in the front passenger seat, but his head was down, and he didn't wave back. She wasn't upset with him, though. She knew what was going on. He was embarrassed. Embarrassed by his father and maybe, she thought, maybe embarrassed that he didn't stand up to him.

Libro

I knew it would be unpleasant at Hobart's house. It's good Hobart has a real friend, but at some point, he's going to have to stand up to his father.

I don't envy him.

I suppose this is all part of the Imaginer's "themes," along with Lily starting a new school, yada yada yada. Don't forget the bully. How could we, much as we'd like to? What about Skylar? And Dunya? Why would they be mentioned if their stories weren't important?

The Imaginer's job is to take all of these disparate story threads and weave them into something cohesive that makes sense, and feels like a warm, cozy blanket when you're done. I always think, *Ha! Good luck to her!* Because I never think she can actually do it.

To be fair (to me), sometimes she doesn't think so, either. Sometimes she does fail, but that's what revisions are for. She goes through many. Trust me. Sometimes I yawn and think, *No, this one's not working*, and she eventually agrees with me. Other times, I will admit, she comes up with an idea that makes me rail, "What on earth are you thinking?" but then, somehow, it works.

Chapter 10

"Class!" Miss Chase yelled on Monday morning, trying to get their attention. "Apparently, someone erased Ryan's statistics project from the whiteboard."

"That was mean," Hobart said.

Lily felt her face grow hot.

"Yeah, and it was important!" Ryan said.

"I'm so sorry," Miss Chase said.

It was not important! Lily wanted to say. *It was cruel!*

"Brady saw who did it, too!" Ryan said.

Lily sank down in her seat.

"Brady?" Miss Chase said.

Lily glanced out of the corner of her eye and saw Brady squirm in his chair. He looked at Lily briefly, then looked away, before Miss Chase said, "Come see me after class, please, Brady."

Lily spent the rest of math class shaking. Was she going to get in trouble? But surely once Miss Chase knew, Ryan would be the one getting in trouble.

She collected her books slowly at the end of class because she knew Miss Chase would want to talk to her.

After Brady stopped briefly at Miss Chase's desk, then ran from the room, Miss Chase asked her, "Lily? Can you explain why you erased the board?"

"Because it wasn't a school project. Ryan and his friends were keeping a tally of the number of days in a row that Skylar wore the same jeans. They were just being mean!"

Miss Chase looked away. "Oh, I see. Well, um, I'll talk to him, but it's complicated. Ryan's family is donating a lot of money for a football team and coach."

"Oh," Lily mumbled, leaving the classroom feeling deflated. If a teacher couldn't stand up to a bully, where did that leave the kids?

In social studies, Mrs. Barry distributed snacks, like she always did. This time it was fruit strips, which Lily ordinarily liked, but she didn't have any appetite. She handed several to Skylar at the next table, who eagerly took them, whispering, "Thanks."

Toward the end of class, Mrs. Barry stood at the whiteboard. "Okay, people, let's go over your ideas—and we're picking at least one—to make our new immigrant students feel welcome. How about the after-school club?"

A girl groaned. "We're all too busy," she said as others agreed. "I don't have time for homework as it is. Mrs. Barry, maybe you'd consider not giving us—"

"Not a chance, Kelly, but nice try. Okay, so during school might be better. How about the buddy system idea?"

"I don't know," Samantha said. "Then they're, like, stuck with one person and what if it's a weird person?"

Mrs. Barry rolled her eyes. "Nobody's 'weird,' Samantha."

A boy waved his hand. "I think the welcome table in the cafeteria is the best idea." His vote was met with a lot of approvals.

"Okay," Mrs. Barry said. "How would you go about creating that?"

"Put a sign on a table that says 'Welcome,'" Ryan said.

Some kids snickered.

"In what languages?" Mrs. Barry asked.

"Whatever," Ryan said.

"All right, Ryan, we'll let you be the one to find out how many whatever languages there need to be, and then make the sign."

"What?" Ryan said.

Now more kids snickered.

"And who would like to organize a roster for people to sit at this table?"

"What people?" Samantha said.

"Hosts," said Zoey, adding "duh" under her breath.

"Right, hosts. It's not very welcoming if no one is there to welcome them."

Ava raised her hand. "I'll do that!"

Lily wondered how Ava, who made fun of Skylar for wearing the same jeans four days in a row, could care about a project like this.

"Great," Mrs. Barry said. "Now, quickly, before the bell rings, new topic. Who would be interested in joining a Geo-Bee club?" She briefly explained the National Geographic bee and how they'd practice together, then compete for one person to represent their school and maybe, eventually, their state.

Several kids raised their hands. Lily did not, even though Mrs. Barry looked directly at her.

As they filed out of class, Mrs. Barry called Lily back. "You could be a big help to the GeoBee team."

"I'm not sure I'm ready. . . ." Lily's voice trailed off.

Mrs. Barry nodded and was quiet for a moment. "Sometimes it's good for us to do things that are familiar when everything else is so . . . unfamiliar. Would you give it some thought?"

Lily said she would. It wasn't really a lie. She would consider it, even though she already knew her answer was going to be no. She loved geography, and Dad said she could've made it to state, and maybe nationals, but she didn't want to get onstage and face a crowd of people who would all be staring at her and listening to her. She would probably just mess up. Besides, if she wouldn't do the bee for Dad, why on earth would she do it now?

"You were the one who erased it?" Hobart knocked his metal water bottle, fortunately capped, onto the table with a clang. "Why did you do that? It was an important project!"

"No. It wasn't," Lily hissed. "They were keeping track of how many days in a row Skylar wore the same pair of jeans. And they were assuming they were never washed."

"Huh? I don't get it."

Lily kept her voice low since Skylar was at the next table. "Just to be mean. Just to make fun of him." Lily felt her heart beating fast. "Maybe his family doesn't have the money to buy a bunch of clothes."

"Skylar's a really nice kid. How can they—"

Hobart stopped and narrowed his eyes when he saw Brady carrying his tray toward Ryan's table. "And Brady told on you. . . . Hey, Brady!"

Brady hesitated, looking toward Ryan, who was deep in conversation. He turned to Hobart but didn't move.

Hobart stalked over to him, talking fast and pointing to Lily. Brady hung his head until Ryan yelled, "Get over here, Brady!"

Brady headed to his table, but Hobart followed him and as they passed her, Lily heard the conversation.

"No, seriously," Hobart was insisting, "why do you hang out with Ryan?"

Brady paused, looking down at his tray. "It's just . . . easier."

"Easier isn't better! Or right!"

"So?" Brady said, half-heartedly.

"What do you mean, so? So, it's wrong!"

Brady raised his head enough to look at Lily. "Sorry," he muttered, before turning and trudging over to his table.

Hobart sat down with an exasperated sigh. "It wasn't much of an apology but at least he said it."

"It's fine, Hobart. I almost feel sorry for him."

"What!"

"It seems like he feels stuck or doesn't know how to get out of that group."

Hobart looked over at Brady. "I can't believe we used to be best friends."

"Poor Brady," Lily said.

"Why? They're all mean!"

She sighed. "I know."

"I'm glad you told me what was happening because I was going to help in the next study! I would've been participating in something mean. I wonder what they were going to count next."

Lily couldn't help it. She found herself staring at Hobart's bow tie, then quickly looking away.

"What?"

"Nothing," she said too fast.

Hobart put his hand to his collar. "Oh. Wait. My bow tie?"

Lily couldn't look at him.

"Maybe I shouldn't wear it anymore."

"You don't have to change because of them."

Hobart shrugged and said, almost talking to himself, "I guess I could decide what I wear."

"Don't you always decide what you wear?"

"No. My mom does."

Lily wasn't sure what to say.

Hobart could tell. "Well, doesn't your mom make you wear a dress every day?"

"No. I just like dresses. They're comfortable. And if you wear bike shorts underneath, it doesn't matter if it's windy or you forget to wear shorts on PE days."

"Oh. My grandmother says when she was in school, girls had to wear dresses. They weren't allowed to wear pants or shorts. You would've liked that."

"No, I wouldn't. I'd hate for someone to tell me I couldn't wear something. I want to make the choice to wear a dress."

Hobart looked at her dress. "I'm going to try that."

"Hobart, if you wear a dress, people will make fun of

you. I mean, they shouldn't, but—"

"I'm not going to wear a dress! I mean, wearing something that I want to wear."

"Good!" Lily said, smiling and hoping that it wouldn't be something that got him teased.

Libro

Of course, he'll be teased because it's something differ-ent. That's one of the things bullies glom onto, isn't it? Anything that's different. They don't like different. Even if different ends up being exactly the same as them.

I think we can predict that Ryan will not be kind. In fact, I heard the Imaginer banging away in the kitchen downstairs, and now she is stomping up the stairs into the attic—always preceded by a large mug of coffee, as if it's leading the way and she's following it.

Gulping coffee. Fingers on keyboard. Sighs. And now stretching over that yoga ball. . . . It is not a pretty sight. Be grateful you only have words to see. Or, hopefully, you'll have words, given that the Imaginer seems to be in pondering mode at the moment.

The only thing worse than the dillydallying of pondering is the research trips. Crikey! Is it really necessary to go to schools, talk with teachers, visit with people from other cultures, ask questions of the military, play with dogs? Well, yes, the dog part I'll allow.

Ah, but there is an amusing part to the Imaginer, although I suspect it's unintended. Acting. Yes, without any acting training. Hilarious. She will jump around the room, yell, be two characters having a conversation, wear unusual outfits, all of which is like watching a B movie.

Thankfully, her characters can act better than she can.

Chapter 11

Hobart, wearing a huge hockey jersey, met Lily in front of her house for the walk to school. He held his arms out, but the ends of the sleeves still covered his hands and hung down several inches. "How do you like it?"

"I didn't think you were a hockey fan," Lily said.

"I'm not, but I told my dad I was going to order one, and he got so excited he said he'd pay for it and I could wear his until the kid size comes in. Do you think it'll make me popular?"

"A hockey jersey?"

"Yeah, a lot of the cool kids wear them. Even Ryan wears one sometimes, so he won't be able to make fun of me."

Lily wasn't sure about that, particularly when Hobart tripped over the hem of the too-long jersey.

She started to help him up, but he popped up quickly, saying, "I'm okay!"

Lily dreaded what the boys at school would say to Hobart.

Ryan didn't waste any time. As soon as they entered homeroom, he called out, "Hey, Ho-fart, you wearing your daddy's hockey jersey?"

Hobart grinned. "Yeah!"

Ryan imitated him, squeaking, "Yeah," and making odd laughing sounds that weren't like Hobart's laugh at all. "It makes you look even smaller than you are."

Hobart's grin disappeared.

Lily wanted to say something but instead just gave Ryan a glare that he didn't see.

Hobart shrugged. "I'll only wear this a few days until I get mine in the mail." He sighed. "I just want everyone to like me."

"I don't think it's possible to make everyone like you, Hobart," Lily replied quietly.

"Wow," Hobart said, "that hurts my feelings."

"No, I mean, no one can make everyone like them. We're all different so some people aren't going to like the type of person you are."

Hobart sat down at his desk. "Maybe no one likes the type of person I am."

"I like you," Lily said.

"What do you like about me?"

"You're friendly. You're kind. You're upbeat. You're fun. You're accepting. You even accepted me."

"Why wouldn't I accept you?"

"See? That's why I like you!"

"So . . . why don't other people like me?"

"I bet a lot of people like you, Hobart."

"It doesn't feel like it."

Lily thought for a moment. "Maybe people don't know enough about you."

Hobart gave her a sideways glance.

"My dad used to say, the more people know about a person, the less they can hate them."

The chimes rang for math, but Hobart looked like he was still thinking about that.

And the more Lily thought about it, the more she thought she was right and wanted to do something about it.

Lily was still getting used to the alternating schedule. English was only Tuesdays and Thursdays, but at least it was a long class. And Hobart was in it. And Ryan was not. Most of all, the teacher, Mrs. Sanchez, was awesome. She reminded Lily of Dad, or at least the way Dad used to teach. Fun, yet challenging. Lily would've felt that way even if she hadn't just gotten her book report back with such a glowing note from Mrs. Sanchez: *Lily, I think this is the best writing I've ever seen from a sixth grader! It's a pleasure having you in my class. Keep up the great work!*

She wished her dad could see her assignment. He used to say it'd be fun to work on an article together. Lily fingered her charm bracelet and wished, again, that she hadn't told him politics was boring.

"No, that's boring!" a girl said, startling Lily. It almost felt like she was hearing herself.

"Yeah," a boy added, "Shakespeare is ancient history."

Mrs. Sanchez smiled. "Nevertheless, I think you'll find that *A Midsummer Night's Dream* is a lot of fun. We're going to start the play in the first half of block, then move on to poetry."

Despite her classmates' groans, Lily knew already that it was a fun play. She had read it with her father. He had great voices for the different characters, even Helena and Titania, and made silly faces. He'd made her read aloud the part of Hermia.

Mrs. Sanchez assigned roles to various kids. Lily kept her head down so she wouldn't be called on. It was hard not to compare her classmates with Dad, which wasn't fair because he was a grown-up and had a lot of practice doing great voices, given how many books he'd read to her ever since she could remember. Listening to the girl who read Hermia's part, Lily felt, secretly, that she could play the role better—not that she wanted to, but she'd improved a lot with Dad's coaching. She'd gotten into it so much that Dad said she should try out for a youth production at the local theater. She'd balked, but he'd said that he could easily see her on the stage. Lily couldn't even picture that. Dad had reiterated how important it was for her to use her voice, which reminded her that she was supposed to be Striving for Five. She was ashamed that she hadn't even done one yet.

Lily realized she hadn't been paying attention, again, because everyone was getting out their journals, and Mrs. Sanchez was pointing to a poem by William Carlos Williams she'd written on the whiteboard, and telling them to use it as inspiration to write a poem about something that had meaning to them.

Hobart raised his hand. "Can it be something you want but don't have yet?"

"Sure," said Mrs. Sanchez.

"*In* the *house!*" Hobart pumped his fist and Lily knew he was writing about curling. She decided that it could also be about something you wanted but couldn't have anymore.

As she listened to students read their poems aloud, Lily realized she'd misunderstood the assignment. Everyone wrote about a thing. She had written—or tried to write—about her father. And most of their poems were funny. Hers ended up being too sad. She looked down at her words.

I'm trying, Dad, but
Strive for Five, and everything else,
would be easier
if you were here. . . .

She wouldn't want to read her poem aloud, anyway.
Mrs. Sanchez made you stand up, which was almost as bad
as being onstage.

"I'll go!" Hobart said, and stood up next to his desk.

This Is Just to Say

I knocked your stone
out of the ring
where it sat

and which you were probably
counting on giving you
more points

Forgive me,
but I'm not really sorry
just like Mr. Williams
wasn't sorry about
eating those plums

The class, and Mrs. Sanchez, laughed. "Exactly," she said. "I think you captured the essence of that poem, Hobart. He wasn't sorry at all, was he?"

Hobart followed Lily out of class. "That was fun! What did you write about?"

Lily wouldn't have minded telling Hobart, but thinking about her dad at that moment made her throat dry and sore. She knew that if she tried to speak, tears might start. She stood frozen for a moment watching Hobart's grin fade and his forehead wrinkle. Finally, she shook her head and scurried to the nearest restroom. Locking herself in a stall, she cried into her arm, as quietly as she could.

Afterward, she wiped her face with a wet paper towel and felt a little better. Still, she really didn't feel like rejoining the day. It would be so much easier if she could just be at home.

She was surprised to find Hobart waiting for her outside the girls' room.

He examined her face. "Are you sick?"

She shook her head.

"You sure you don't want to go to the nurse?"

"No, I'm just sad. She can't fix it."

"It's a he, actually. The nurse. But I get what you mean. I'll walk you to class."

"But you don't have PE now."

"I know. But I can still walk with you."

"Thanks, Hobart," she whispered.

Hobart didn't say anything more. He didn't need to. It was comforting just having a friend by her side.

Thursday meant late lunch, but at least it was still with Hobart. Lily looked for him as she entered the cafeteria. She smiled when she saw him, swinging his lunch bag in one hand and running his other hand, or rather, his adult-sized jersey sleeve, along the cafeteria wall.

Then she saw Ryan. He held up a big red apple in his fist and was aiming it at Hobart.

Lily looked frantically for the Hammer. Thursday! He wasn't here!

Ryan drew his arm back like a baseball pitcher and brought it forward. It felt as if everything was happening in slow motion, except that in a split second Hobart would be hit.

What happened next shocked even Lily.

"MANITOBA TUCK!" she screamed.

Hobart dropped to the floor as the rotten apple smacked against the wall above him and red and white sludge dripped down.

Hobart popped up and stared at the wall for a moment before turning to look around the cafeteria until he spotted Lily.

"That was awesome!" he yelled to Lily, and only then did she realize that she was the one who had shouted.

Slowly, she grinned. She'd used her voice when it really counted. Loudly! In front of everyone. Her very first Strive for Five.

Hobart was grinning, too, as they watched a teacher leading Ryan out of the cafeteria amid a chorus of *Oooohs*.

"That's Mr. Lindsay, my social studies teacher," Hobart said as he joined her. "He's cool!"

After school, Lily went up to her room and took the state charm out of the silver box. She attached it to her charm bracelet, whispering, "I did it, Dad." She admired it on her wrist and almost showed Mom but decided to wait. Mom had a habit of getting excited, almost like a cheerleader, and she'd probably ask Lily every single day if she'd managed a second Strive for Five. For now, it was just between Lily and Dad.

Libro

Kudos, huzzahs, and ululations to Lily for yelling, "MANITOBA TUCK!"

That. Was. Brilliant.

I daresay you did not see that coming.

Neither did Lily.

Neither did the Imaginer.

I know, because I saw an earlier draft and it was the Hammer who yelled it.

Fortunately, Mr. Hammer took the Imaginer aside and explained that this was Lily's story, not his.

Ah, sweet revision, how I love the way you add depth and meaning!

And now . . . sigh.

Much as it pains me, I will say this for Hobart's father,

though it is all I will say for him: Mr. Hall is generous. He offered to help with handyman tasks at Lily's house for free. And he is paying for the hockey jersey Hobart was willing to buy himself.

There, I said it. I suspect there will be no need to say anything further on this matter.

Read on.

Chapter 12

Lily and Hobart raised their eyebrows at each other as they listened to the arguing in the hallway outside Principal Cooper's office on Monday morning. Stopping at Hobart's locker, they couldn't help but hear the conversation.

"I will not have my son being called a bully, as if he's the only one who's ever tossed food in a cafeteria or kept track of someone's hygiene, or lack thereof," a woman was saying.

"Ryan's mom," Hobart whispered, though Lily had already guessed.

"No one is saying that, Mrs. King—" the principal began, but Ryan's mom interrupted.

"They might as well have! As a matter of fact, I think

it's *my* son who's being bullied. I'm going to stay with him through lunch today. Take me to his first class."

Lily and Hobart lagged behind Mrs. Cooper and Mrs. King.

"Can you believe it?" Hobart said.

Lily shook her head.

When they reached homeroom, Miss Chase stood out in the hall looking at Mrs. King and Mrs. Cooper. The principal shrugged and gave Miss Chase a sheepish smile.

In turn, Miss Chase gave Ryan's mom a grimace that Lily guessed was trying to be a smile. "You're welcome to sit in."

"Of course I'm welcome! I pay taxes, not to mention all the extra funds we're donating to this place."

Hobart discreetly rolled his eyes at Lily as they made their way to their desks.

"Oh, here, Mom," Ryan said, "let me get you a chair." He took Miss Chase's chair from her desk and wheeled it to the back of the room next to his desk. He gave a fake smile to Miss Chase as she entered the room, then grinned at the class.

Lily and Hobart looked at each other.

Mrs. King sat down, then bent over and picked up Ryan's hoodie and a pencil. "Here, sweetie."

"Thanks, Mom," Ryan said in such a cloying voice it made Lily want to throw up.

"Okay, um, class," Miss Chase said, "let's get out our pencils and workbooks for math."

"Mom," Ryan said loudly, "do you have a *pen* I could borrow?"

"You don't have one, sweetie?" She rummaged in her purse.

"Miss Chase likes us to use pencils. So we can erase. Because she says we make a lot of mistakes."

"No," Miss Chase protested, "it's just that, well, it's math, so it's—"

"Pencils are for babies," Ryan's mom snapped. "These kids are going into middle school next year. They can use pens." She handed a fancy gold one to Ryan.

Miss Chase swallowed hard as several other kids pulled out pens.

Lily held firmly onto her pencil and hoped Miss Chase noticed her support.

"Knowing this school," Mrs. King muttered, "someone probably stole your pen."

Lily turned and stared at the woman.

"Do you have a problem?" Mrs. King said to her.

Lily quickly turned back around, her face burning, and looked at her workbook, but she distinctly heard Ryan's mom say, "We'll get you into Westminster for sure next year. At least maybe *you'll* have a chance to turn out right."

Lily gritted her teeth. Westminster was a private boys'

school where rich kids went. Was Mrs. King saying that kids who went to public school didn't have a chance to turn out right? And what did she mean by *We'll get you in*? You had to have good grades to get into Westminster. Had Ryan tried and failed? And now his parents were going to buy his way in?

Lily startled when a cell phone rang loudly. Ryan's mom fished in her huge leopard-skin bag. "I hear you. It's in here somewhere."

To Lily's disbelief, she answered the call right there in the classroom. "No, I'm not paying for six. I only wanted five."

Miss Chase cleared her throat. Smiling, she said in a loud whisper, "Would you mind taking that outside?"

"Fine. Yes. I'll take it all the way to the principal's office!" Mrs. King stormed out of the classroom, then popped her head back in, the phone to her ear. "Hold on a second!" She looked at Ryan. "The fabric came in for the sofa cushions so I can't stay—" She gave an exasperated sigh. "I said hold on!" She closed the door behind her.

There was an awkward silence before Miss Chase said, "Okay, let's get back to ratios."

Lily didn't understand Mrs. King. She stole a glance at Ryan, who was hunched over his desk, and almost felt sorry for him.

* * *

In the cafeteria, Lily noticed a table with Welcome written in many languages. She also noticed that several popular kids, like Ava and Samantha, were sitting there, chatting with each other. Lily had never even seen the volunteer sign-up sheet that Ava was in charge of. A boy holding an *English for Everyone* book hesitated at the table, but when Samantha and Ava were too busy talking to notice him, he kept walking. Lily winced. They were not being welcoming at all. In fact, they were arguing.

"Our neighbor wears a turban so that means he's Muslim," Samantha said.

"But you said he's from India, so he has to be Hindu," Ava countered.

"No, Hindus come from Pakistan. The two biggest countries with Muslims are India and Africa."

Lily groaned inside at the same time as she heard a groan behind her.

She turned to see Mrs. Barry with a hand on her forehead. "Oh, boy, people, do we need a geography club. First of all, Africa is not a country. It's a continent of many countries. And you're mixed up with your religious assumptions." She sighed. "Lily, can you enlighten them?"

Lily didn't really want to because she knew it would only make Samantha mad, but she noticed Dunya standing near the table now, watching, and she didn't want her to think she thought the way these girls did. She took a deep breath. "Not everyone from India is Hindu, nor is everyone in Pakistan Muslim. Those are just the predominant religions."

"I was right," Ava said, sitting up straight and crossing her arms.

"Only sort of," Mrs. Barry pointed out.

"Your neighbor," Lily said to Samantha, "is probably Sikh."

"*Seek?* What do you mean *seek?*"

"It's a religion. Most Sikhs live in India but some live here. Is his last name Singh?"

Samantha looked at Ava, then at Lily. "Do you know him?"

"All Sikh men are given the last name Singh to use if they want. It means *lion*. Women can take the last name Kaur, which means *princess*, or maybe *prince*, I can't remember. The point is that women are equal to men."

Samantha stared at Lily for a long moment. "Are you, like, Wikipedia or something?"

Mrs. Barry put her hands on her hips. "It's called being informed. Maybe a geography club, and participating in the GeoBee, would help." She raised her eyebrows hopefully at Lily. "That was very impressive."

Lily looked away.

Hobart walked up to Lily as Mrs. Barry was saying to Ava and Samantha, "We all have a great opportunity to learn from our newcomers."

Ryan stood behind Mrs. Barry, made an annoyed face, and put his hands on his hips, imitating her. Samantha bit her lip to keep from laughing.

After Mrs. Barry left, Ryan, still imitating her, said, "Or maybe our *newcomers* can leave so they stop living on welfare and being criminals."

Samantha smirked, but Ava frowned as Ryan sauntered off, calling after him, "Thanks a lot for *not* making the welcome sign, Ryan!"

Lily quickly looked around for Dunya and was relieved to see she'd already sat down and hadn't heard what Ryan said.

As Lily and Hobart walked to their lunch table, Hobart said, "That's not true. Immigrants actually help the economy and even create more jobs."

"I know."

"And they pay taxes, but they don't get to have any help, even with food, until they've been here at least five years."

"I know," Lily said as they sat at their table.

"Also, Melissa says they're not terrorists, and she knows because she's a soldier actually *in* Iraq. She's met some of the people who are coming to the U.S." He finished taking his lunch out of his box and turned to Lily. "Plus, they don't commit crimes as much as the rest of us do."

"Hobart?"

"What?"

"How did you know all that?"

He grinned. "I was finding out the *why!*" His grin fell away. "I printed it out and left it on my dad's TV chair for him to read."

"What did he think?"

Hobart shrugged. "He dumped it in the kitchen trash. Except the email from Melissa that said hi to all of us."

Lily didn't know what to say. She thought quite a few things, though, like *Why would Mr. Hall do that? Wouldn't he want to learn? Wouldn't he at least want to know what mattered to Hobart, even if he disagreed, and talk with him about it?*

When they left the cafeteria, Lily took one last look at the welcome table. She realized that, even though she wasn't from a different country, she couldn't have broken through that wall of popularity. In fact, she wouldn't have a friend if Hobart hadn't befriended her. That was how it should happen—the buddy system. Lily realized she needed to be a buddy to someone . . . once she got up the nerve.

That night, Lily told her mom more about Mrs. King's visit—how she picked up after Ryan, gave him a pen, said people at their school must've stolen his, and was rude to Miss Chase—ending with her storming out to the principal's office.

Mom slammed the cabinet door and put a can of baked beans on the counter hard. "That mother should be *sent* to the principal's office!" She shook her head. "And that boy is never going to grow up. He will be a spoiled brat his whole life. We're supposed to be raising adults, not children."

"His parents give a lot of money to the school. They're starting a football team, with a coach, even."

"So? Does that mean no one can cross her?" Mom snorted.

"Yes."

"You're kidding, right?"

Lily shook her head.

Mom let out a loud sigh. "For goodness' sake."

Lily also told her mom Mrs. King's comment about getting Ryan into Westminster.

Mom looked at Lily, her jaw set. "He's going to end up like my student whose mother came to college with him and they're sharing an apartment. She writes all his notecards while he's out partying. Probably writes his papers, too, but I can't prove it. He wouldn't be passing the class if she weren't doing so much work for him."

Mom shucked the corn, muttering to herself. She turned to Lily again. "You know I love you, right? The reason I don't do all those things is that I want you to be able to take care of yourself. If I make all your decisions and do everything for you, how will you ever learn?"

"I know, Mom." Sometimes, Lily felt it would be nice if Mom would do things like make her bed and do her laundry, but mostly Lily liked that her mom trusted her and treated her like, well, sort of like a grown-up, or a "growing up" as Dad used to say.

"As an instructor myself, I feel sorry for Miss Chase."

"She's new," Lily said, "and doesn't really know how to handle the class."

"It sounds like she needs help. Do you want me to talk with her? Or to the principal to let her know Miss Chase needs some help?"

Uh-oh, Lily thought. When Mom saw something she thought was wrong, she wanted to make it right, and she wasn't quiet about it like Dad was.

"No, Mom, it's fine."

"Are you sure? It's back-to-school night tonight. I could bring it up."

Lily had forgotten all about back-to-school night. "No, really. Please—"

"Okay, fine," Mom said, and then gave her wry smile. "I'll just talk with your teachers about my wonderful daughter and how lucky they are to have her in class."

Lily groaned.

Later, Mom returned from back-to-school night with Lily's favorite hazelnut gelato, plunking the container on the kitchen counter. "Well, I like Mrs. Barry and Mrs.

Sanchez, in particular, and I would say that even if they hadn't both gushed over you, and said how mature and talented you are. They both wish you'd speak up in class more, though."

"Dad already taught me everything, so classes are easy," Lily said, which was true, but didn't address the "speak up in class" part that Mom was referring to.

Mom took down two bowls from the cabinet and started to open the ice cream, but stopped to stare into space. "I see what you mean about Miss Chase. I think she needs reinforcement. We'll have to do something about that."

Lily groaned inwardly. "I'll get the spoons. Do you want me to scoop?"

"What? Oh, okay. Do you know that Mrs. Barry would love for you to help her start a GeoBee club?"

"Uh-huh," Lily said, focusing on scooping the ice cream.

"I hope you'll think about that."

"I will."

"Back to Miss Chase—"

"Mom, if I promise to take care of that, will you drop it?"

Mom crossed her arms and looked at Lily. "What do you have in mind?"

Lily shrugged. "I don't know yet—but something."

Mom frowned.

"You always say I need to find my voice."

"That's true. I do." Mom raised her eyebrows. "And notice your teachers said that, too."

"I know, Mom."

"Okay, I'll give you some time, but let me know if you need any help."

Lily knew she needed a lot of help with Ryan. How was she going to handle that situation? She had no idea what she was going to do. She knew, though, that Dad would be proud of her for stepping up to the plate.

Libro

Regarding bullies. Underneath, they are scared and fragile—yes, fragile. To counteract that, they become blustery, brutal, and bombastic to acquire some followers. After all, it's an effort to make real friends.

And a risk. Someone might not like you. Someone may say something mean. Someone might reject you or laugh at you. News flash: That happens to everyone from time to time. Still, it is worth taking that risk to find a true friend.

But to do so, you must be brave. Look at Lily. True, Hobart was the one who stuck his neck out to make friends with her, but Lily is brave, too . . . just watch.

Chapter 13

*L*ily thought hard about what to do to help Miss Chase or stop Ryan from being disruptive, preferably both. By Wednesday, Lily remembered that Mrs. Barry had said she'd be happy to answer any questions. So Lily forced herself to ask.

When Mrs. Barry marched into homeroom, Lily suppressed a grin. Mrs. Barry was there because of her. It made Lily feel like she had an ally.

"Mr. King," Mrs. Barry said, pointing at Ryan, "backpack in the aisle, tripping hazard." She looked down the rows of desks and her eyebrows shot up. "Seriously? Books go *on* the shelf, tablets go *on* the cart, not on the floor next to it where they can get rolled over. Food trash goes . . . let's see . . . oh, yes, *in the trash*. Come on, people! You have two minutes before the bell for math. Go!"

Most people jumped up and put things away. Ryan still hadn't even picked up his backpack.

Mrs. Barry called out to him. "Ryan, I'm sure you're just as mature as any of these other students, so you can clean up after yourself, too."

Ryan kicked his backpack under his seat with a sneer.

The chimes rang for math class and Miss Chase said, "Today we're going to apply ratios to *word* problems."

"Oh, goodie, *word* problems," Ryan said, imitating Miss Chase as she started the first example.

"Excuse me, Ryan," Mrs. Barry said. "Are you actually talking while Miss Chase is talking? That's disrespectful and you know better." She folded her arms and looked at the students. "Are you all happy with the way class is going?"

No one answered.

"How much math you're learning?"

Now there were embarrassed giggles.

"So you won't mind being behind when you get to middle school?"

The giggles died down.

"I do!" Zoey said. "But *some* people won't stop talking."

"Nerd," Ryan muttered.

Zoey turned in her seat. "Yes, actually, and I'm proud of it."

Lily envied how tough Zoey was. She wasn't big or popular. She was just gutsy. And smart, or at least cared about learning. Zoey could probably have done Strive for Five in kindergarten.

Mrs. Barry wrapped up her lecture and stayed for a few minutes of math class, staring at the class, mainly Ryan, before leaving.

After social studies, when all the students had left, Lily went up to Mrs. Barry, who was erasing the whiteboard. "Thank you for coming to homeroom."

"I'm glad you came to see me, Lily. I didn't realize Miss Chase was having quite such a hard time." Mrs. Barry put the eraser on the tray and turned to Lily. "It's good to see you speaking up for things you care about. Impressive!"

"Thank you," Lily said, feeling her face grow hot. She had spoken up, hadn't she? And maybe it wasn't in front of a crowd, but it was *for* a crowd—the kids in her class. Dad would've said she was being like one of the grassroots politicians he covered. Lily almost grinned.

"I'm proud of you," Mrs. Barry said. It was exactly what her father would've said.

In fact, she could almost hear him saying it was time to add the United States charm to her bracelet because this was the second Strive for Five!

When Lily got to the cafeteria, she saw Ryan lean over Dunya, who was sitting by herself, and say something, grin, then leave. Lily hesitated, but finally walked up to her table. "Are you okay?"

Dunya nodded quickly. She wiped her eyes with a napkin.

"Was it . . . Ryan?" Lily knew it was a silly question. Of course it was Ryan.

Dunya waved her hand dismissively and said something softly, but Lily thought she heard the word *ignore*.

Lily gritted her teeth. She wasn't sure ignoring Ryan would take care of the problem, though she didn't know what to do about it. She also realized that maybe she'd helped Miss Chase—or Mrs. Barry would—but she hadn't solved the Ryan problem yet. She would still need to work on that.

Dunya was unzipping her lunch box. Lily felt awkward standing there staring at her, so she mumbled, "I'm sorry," and turned away.

She froze when she saw Ryan at Skylar's table and Skylar hunched over his lunch bag, sandwich in his hands. She couldn't hear all of what Ryan was saying, just some words like *baby*, *loser*, and *Wakanda forever* in a mocking tone. She knew exactly how Skylar felt. His eyes were fixed on the table, and although he'd stopped chewing a bite of food, he still hadn't swallowed.

Why didn't she do anything? Dad would've done something. It was easier for an adult, though.

Even when Ryan walked off to his table, Lily still wished she could do something. She remembered how Dad had always invited kids to join them for lunch when they were at a museum or homeschool event. Sometimes, she didn't want him to. But almost always, it ended up being okay, even fun. Why hadn't she thought of it before?

Lily put her lunch bag down. "Hobart, you need to ask Skylar to eat with us. It's silly for him to be sitting alone."

Hobart smiled. "Good idea!"

She watched him dash over to Skylar and knew what she had to do. She took a deep breath, turned, and walked back the way she came.

"Hi," she said to Dunya. Her voice sounded loud in her ears, and she could feel her heart beating, but she couldn't stop now. "Would you like to join us at our table?"

Dunya looked up at her and smiled. "Yes, thank you." She stood and grabbed her lunch, following Lily.

Lily breathed a sigh of relief. After she made introductions, there was an awkward silence. It was uncomfortable sitting with someone you didn't know and couldn't really talk to. Or it would've been, without Hobart.

"Here! Try some!" Hobart passed out brownie bites to everyone. "My mom baked them."

Skylar scarfed his down eagerly.

Dunya took a tentative bite. "I like it!" She opened a container of small sausage links and showed it to Hobart. "Try some."

"Thanks!" Hobart popped one in his mouth.

His eyes grew wide as he chewed, and he opened his mouth, breathing fast. He grabbed the top of his metal water bottle, unscrewing it quickly, and started gulping. Dropping the empty bottle on the table with a clang, he squeaked, "It's really good!"

Lily couldn't help laughing. Hobart joined her, water coming out of his eyes. Even Skylar grinned.

"I am sorry," Dunya said. "It is too . . . seasoned? You do not like it?"

"Too hot. Spicy," Hobart said, sticking his tongue out and fanning it with his hand, "but I can tell it's good underneath."

"My grandmother makes them," Dunya explained. "She likes spicy. My mother says her tongue does not . . . taste well because she is *vieille*—I mean, old."

"Is that French?" Lily asked.

"Yes. Sometimes I use French words when I am trying to say English."

"French? I thought you'd speak Arabic."

"Yes, Arabic, of course, also."

"*Three* languages?" Hobart smacked his forehead. "Okay, I feel stupid now!"

Skylar smacked his forehead, too, and both boys laughed.

Lily and Dunya grinned at each other, shaking their heads.

"My brother is learning faster because he is young. He

has many friends already. And he is on a soccer team."

"Does he know about curling?" Hobart said.

"Curling?"

Hobart launched into an explanation as Dunya tried to keep up. "Oh, no! He cannot throw stones in the house."

"No, it's not real stones in a real house, it's—oh! There's the Hammer. He's late today. I have to go say hi. I'll explain more later."

Skylar followed Hobart to the Hammer.

"Curling is a little confusing," Lily said to Dunya, who nodded in agreement.

They were quiet for a minute. Lily tried to think of what to say. Mom always said to ask people about themselves to start a conversation. "Do you like to read?"

Dunya pulled a book out of her backpack and showed it to Lily. "We are learning to read this."

"*A Crooked Kind of Perfect*? I love that book!"

"Dunya," a curly-haired teacher said approaching their table, "it's your tutoring time—"

"Oh! Sorry, Miss Hinojosa!" Dunya said, grabbing her book and backpack and starting to stand.

"No, no, it's okay," the teacher said, gently touching Dunya's shoulder, "I was just going to tell you to stay and chat instead." The woman gave Lily a smile.

"Thank you, Miss Hinojosa." Dunya sat back down. As the teacher walked away, Dunya said, "I like her so much.

She is very kind."

Lily and Dunya spent the last minutes of lunch talking about their favorite parts of the book.

All the while, Lily heard Dad's voice in her head. *Girls make excellent friends.*

She couldn't help smiling. And she'd spoken up, stepped out of her comfort zone, and invited Dunya to join them. That, she knew deserved another Strive for Five, along with getting Mrs. Barry's help. Two in one day! Maybe Dad was-right; maybe it did get easier every time.

That night, Lily showed Mom her charm bracelet. She'd added the United States for going to see Mrs. Barry and North America for inviting Dunya and Skylar to their table.

Mom's eyes widened. "Three!"

Lily nodded, grinning.

"I think this calls for dinner out. Where would you like to go?"

"Really? Um . . . Mexican!"

"And over dinner," Mom said, "I hope you'll share your three successes with me."

Lily was ready now. She wanted to be well into her Strive for Five before she told Mom and Mom got too excited. Three was like a quorum in the city council or school board votes Dad covered—you were already over the hump.

Libro

I do believe Lily has found her voice! I, for one, am delighted. She may still be scared to use it, but she is well on her way to the magic Strive for Five.

Question: When Lily has earned all five charms, is the story over? Is that the be-all and end-all? All of life's problems wrapped up and tied neatly in a bow? She can rest on her laurels? She has reached the pinnacle of success? How many more trite sayings can I spout? Many.

I shall stop, as I trust you will ponder the question.

Hint: The answer is no. But you knew that already, didn't you?

Chapter 14

Hobart had finally received his child-sized hockey jersey and wore it to school proudly on Thursday morning.

"Nice jersey, Ho-fart," Ryan said in homeroom. "Or it would be if you weren't too puny and scared to play hockey!"

Lily watched Hobart shrink down in his desk. He took out his curling book and began to read, or pretend to. Lily desperately wished she could stop Ryan or that Miss Chase would. Unfortunately, the class was only marginally better, despite Mrs. Barry's visit. The main difference was that Zoey now called Ryan out more often on his behavior.

Lily thought about the power of words and how much she loved using them, but also how they could be used so cruelly. She wished there were a way to use words for good and to stand behind them, because Miss Chase mentioned *respect* often and pointed to the word in the front of the room, but that didn't make respect actually happen. And it certainly didn't stop Ryan.

By lunchtime, Lily had an idea. She looked from Hobart, beside her, to Dunya and Skylar across from them.

"Skylar, may I have your lunch bag for a minute?"

Skylar's forehead creased, but he slowly pushed the worn bag across the table to her.

In purple pen, Lily wrote on a sticky note: *It's awesome and mature how you make your own lunch every day!* She put the note on his bag and slid it back over to Skylar.

He read the message and blushed, giving her a shy smile.

"What did she write?" Hobart asked.

Skylar showed him.

"Hey!" Hobart said. "Is that true? Cool!"

Now Skylar's smile was even wider.

Lily took a deep breath, remembering her father's words, *You have good ideas, Lily, you just have to share them.* "You guys, I want to start a campaign of writing notes— nice notes, friendly notes, notes that help people get to know and understand each other better. For example, if kids knew more about Dunya and some of the other new students, maybe they wouldn't"—she didn't want to say *call them terrorists* or *tell them to go home* or any of the other mean things she'd heard from Ryan—"they wouldn't . . ."

"Act like Ryan?" Hobart said.

"Exactly. If we give people information so they understand, then it's harder to be mean. We're really not that different. Like, kids in Iraq play video games, too."

"Especially my little brother," Dunya said, rolling her eyes.

"What about questions?" Hobart said.

"What do you mean?" Lily asked.

"Like your dad asked. To find out the *why*. If you ask people questions, it might make them think, like, *Do you know how many languages Dunya speaks?* or *Can you find El Salvador on a map?* Maybe they'll even want to join that GeoBee club."

Lily stared at him. "How did you know about that? You're not in Mrs. Barry's class."

"Mr. Lindsay told us in social studies. He's the one who asked us where El Salvador was. No one got it. Except Javier because he's from El Salvador. Which is cool. I never knew that! Anyway, Mr. Lindsay said we obviously need a GeoBee team. I'd join except all I know is curling and statistics."

"You don't have to know any geography before you start," Lily said. "The point is to have fun learning about the world."

"Geography has statistics in it," Skylar said, "like population, climate change, stuff like that." When he noticed them all looking at him, he sat on his hands and sank down in his chair. Softly, he added, "Plus, you're smart."

Hobart puffed his cheeks out, trying to hide his grin. "I'll think about it."

Skylar looked over at Lily. "I like your notes idea."

"Me, too," Dunya said, pulling a pen and spiral note-book out of her backpack. "I will write a note now!"

"Me, three!" Hobart agreed. He looked around his place as if wishing pen and paper to appear, so Lily tore a sheet from her notebook and gave him a pen.

Skylar struggled to pull things out of his backpack, items clunking against each other, until he dug down far enough for a notebook and his chewed-up pencil.

Dunya watched him quietly.

After a few minutes, they shared their notes. Lily's note from Dunya read, *You are kind and wise, and you know a lot about different countries!* Lily's mouth dropped open when she saw the beautiful handwriting. "That's awesome." She meant both the writing and the sentiment.

To Hobart, Dunya had written, *Thank you for being a friend. My tutor says I can stay at lunch because talking with friends helps me learn English.*

Lily smiled across the table at Dunya, who smiled shyly back.

"Wow, Dunya," Hobart said, "your writing is like

calligraphy! My mom took a whole class in that. Did you take calligraphy in school?"

"It really is beautiful," Lily added.

"Thank you." Dunya fiddled with her pen. "It is just how I write."

Hobart had written a note to Dunya saying, *I can't believe you speak three languages! You're so smart!* To Skylar, he wrote, *Dude, you're a math genius!*

Hobart looked at Lily and Dunya. "Did you know Skylar is already doing algebra?"

"Algebra?" Dunya's eyes opened wide. "I was only beginning, and I was good at math."

Skylar shrugged his shoulders up. "I just like it. There's always a right answer. No one says you're wrong or stup—" He looked down quickly. "There's always a right answer."

Dunya studied him for a moment before writing in her notebook, carefully tearing out the piece of paper and handing it to Skylar.

After Skylar read it, he swallowed hard and stared at the table. Lily was worried that Dunya might've chosen the wrong words and inadvertently hurt his feelings.

"Can I look?" Hobart asked.

Skylar handed him the note and Lily read over Hobart's shoulder.

Sometimes it is not easy, but you are strong, and it will get better.

"We lived in a refugee camp for a while," Dunya said to no one in particular. "It was not easy. We had to leave our house and drive and then walk a long way to safety. A tent is not a home, though. But we are here now. We only have a bedroom for my parents and a living room, so I sleep on the sofa and my brother sleeps on the floor."

"Really?" Hobart said. "We have an air mattress if you want it."

Dunya waved her hand, shaking her head. "Thank you, but we are fine. My father says that soon he will save enough money to have an apartment with three bedrooms." She looked at Skylar, who was twirling his pencil with his fingers. "It will get better."

"See," said Hobart. "Who knew you lived in a tent? I didn't know. Can one of our notes be: *Ask Dunya about being a refugee?*"

"Maybe she doesn't want to talk about it," Skylar said, barely above a whisper.

"I don't mind," Dunya told Hobart. "It is behind me." She turned to Skylar. "It is easier to talk about when it is behind you."

Lily wanted to say something, but she didn't know what.

Hobart, his forehead wrinkled, looked at Skylar. "Anyway, it helps to have friends, right?"

Lily nodded, and Skylar joined her.

"Well, lookie here," Ryan said, stopping in front of their

table, "it's the table of aliens." He pointed at Lily. "Possibly legal." Then at Dunya. "Definitely illegal." Then Hobart and Skylar. "Aliens from another galaxy."

Lily felt everyone cringe—everyone, that is, except Dunya.

"You are a mean boy," Dunya said, folding her arms and facing him.

"Aw, listen to that, guys, I'm a mean boy!" He and his entourage laughed.

She gave him a cold stare. "Why is this funny?"

Ryan was still grinning but didn't quite seem to know how to respond. "Hi, Ho-fart!"

Lily took some courage from Dunya's behavior and heard herself say, "It's Ho-*bart*."

"Oh, look! Ho-*fart* has girlfriends!"

Lily thought of what her dad had said, and though her voice was shaking and her face felt hot, she said quietly, "Girls make excellent friends."

"True," Dunya said, still giving Ryan her mom stare. "I see you do not have any."

Ryan sauntered off, but Lily couldn't help thinking that he seemed a little awkward. Maybe the positive words at her table had helped her speak out—that and Dunya's bravery. She didn't feel as icky as she usually did after an encounter with Ryan.

"Dunya," Hobart said, "you have the best mom stare ever!"

"I am old for grade six," she explained, "so he is just a little boy. He cannot scare me."

Hobart tilted his head. "How old are you?"

"Almost thirteen."

"Wow," Skylar said, "you're like a big sister."

"I *am* a big sister," Dunya said, "and this stare works for my little brother, too!"

Lily was still watching Ryan and his crew, particularly Brady, who hung back, looking like one of those teenagers she often saw who kept a little distance from their families, like they were almost embarrassed to be part of the group.

"I have another note idea," Lily announced. "It's a question, like you suggested, Hobart. *Why make fun of people when you can be friends?*"

"Yeah," said Hobart, "or *Does it really matter how big or small a person is?* And, *If someone likes a different sport than you, why don't you ask them about it instead of make fun of it?*"

Skylar nodded and whispered, *"Who cares what someone brings for lunch?"*

"*Or what they wear?*" Hobart added.

"*Or,*" Dunya said, "*if they follow a different religion? Or are from another country?*"

"Yes!" Lily said. "All of that!"

They scribbled down their thoughts until the chimes signaled the end of lunch.

Lily hung back with Hobart, as they watched Skylar

leave the cafeteria, and asked Dunya, "How did you know all that about Skylar?"

"I saw in his backpack when he took out his notebook. He has clothes. And cans of food. He cannot use cans of food for lunch. It must be food for his family, from teachers."

Lily thought about how Mrs. Barry always had snacks for them. Was that because of Skylar? And other kids like him?

"My tutor brings in food for all of us," Dunya continued, "but I told her that my family is okay. My parents work all the time."

"How did you know he's living in a tent?" Hobart asked.

Dunya smiled. "I did not say that. But I think he may not be in a stable place, just like a refugee camp, which is . . . What is, a short time, before you move to a stable place?"

"Temporary housing," Lily said.

Dunya nodded. "Yes."

"Whoa," Hobart said, "that's three things I learned today: Javier is from El Salvador, you were in a refugee camp, and"—he looked out the cafeteria door where Skylar had left—"Skylar's having a rough time."

"But what you said is true," Dunya said to Hobart. "He has friends." She smiled at Lily. "This makes all the difference."

Libro

B e kind, for everyone you meet is fighting a hard battle. Socrates said that.

Probably also your mother.

They are both correct.

You wouldn't know from Hobart's happy appearance that he's dealing with bullying at school and at home. You wouldn't know from Lily's quiet manner that she still misses her father terribly or that she has so many ideas. Or what Dunya and Skylar are going through.

You have your battles, too, as does everyone. Wouldn't it be preferable if we helped each other through the day instead of throwing up roadblocks? Even a smile or a kind, supportive word here and there would help.

Incidentally, do you remember I intimated that Dunya

and Skylar were in the story for a reason? Flip back to my earlier remarks if you don't believe me.

See?

Yes, I am wise.

Thank you.

Chapter 15

As they walked Skippy, Lily listened to Hobart's excited chatter over their new project. "I can think of lots more notes. I have to write them all down before I forget, like, *What's making you be a bully? Did you ever think about that?* Because maybe if people really thought about it, they could start changing. I mean, what's the point of being a bully, anyway?"

Hobart kept talking while Lily thought about Ryan, and how she'd spoken up against his bullying. *It's Ho-bart,* she'd actually said. And Dad's line about girls making excellent friends. She never would've thought she could do that. Maybe Strive for Five was truly working. She knew one thing that made it a lot easier to speak up: having friends around you. Now she understood what Dad meant about a "symbiotic" relationship between politicians and their supporters. When the supporters were happy with what the politician was doing, that made the politician feel more empowered.

By the time they got back to Lily's house, her mom was home, typing on her laptop at the kitchen table.

"Mom, is it okay if Hobart stays for a while?"

"Of course," she said, without looking up. "Hobart can stay here forever if he wants."

Hobart grinned.

So did Lily. "Great! We can write some more notes!"

They dumped their backpacks on the couch, leaving just enough room for the two of them to sit and write their notes, dozens of them.

Can you find El Salvador on a map?

Did you know Javier is from El Salvador and understands Spanish?

If a girl wears a head scarf or a boy wears a turban, what are you afraid of?

Indonesia has the largest Muslim population. (It's in Asia, not the Middle East)

Africa is not a country. It's a continent with 54 countries. Can you name 10 of them?

Côte d'Noire produces the most cocoa beans (chocolate!!). Do you know where it is?

Do you believe everything you hear or do you ask why to find out the truth?

What are you adding by being a bully? What's stopping you from stopping?

Do you know what a saola is? Better find out because it's almost extinct!

What sport was played on the moon? (No, really—look it up!)

Where was the beginning of civilization? (If you don't know, ask Dunya!)

"Is this a class project?" Mom asked as she put glasses of water in front of them.

"Nope," said Hobart, "it's all Lily's idea. Write notes to give kids information, and questions so they can find out the *why.*"

"I love that!" Mom beamed at Lily.

"The questions were Hobart's idea."

Hobart grinned while Mom continued beaming.

"Honey, have you spoken with Mrs. Barry lately?"

Lily nodded, still smiling from Mom's approval.

"About the National Geographic bee?" Mom said, her voice rising hopefully at the end.

"Mostly about Miss Chase needing help with math class."

Hobart looked up. "That was you? Whoa. That was smart!" He looked at Mrs. Flippin. "Guess what else? Did you know she asked Dunya to sit at our table at lunch? She's this kid from Iraq."

Mom smiled at Lily. "Yes. That was very brave."

"You think *that* was brave," Hobart said, "she talked back to Ryan—he's a real bully—and stuck up for me!"

Mom's eyebrows raised. "Well," she said, staring at Lily, "with all of that, don't you think you've earned another Strive for Five?"

"What's Strive for Five?" Hobart said.

Mom's eyes widened and she stood up, putting a hand over her mouth.

"It's okay, Mom. I don't mind if Hobart knows." And she didn't. He'd be the first one outside of her parents who knew about Strive for Five, but somehow it seemed perfectly normal that he should be part of their group. She explained, showing him her bracelet with the state, U.S., and North America charms for her first three Strive for Fives. "I'll be right back."

Lily went to her room to add the silver globe, her fourth Strive for Five, showing it to her mom and Hobart when she returned to the living room.

"Cool!" Hobart said. "So now you have four out of five!"

It felt like Mom couldn't stop smiling at her.

"We also asked Skylar to sit at our table," Hobart added, "so now there are four of us. We're a team!"

Lily found herself grinning. They *were* a team. And she had been a part of putting that team together. She hadn't just been dumped in a group or had neighborhood kids include her in a game; she had helped make this happen. In her head, she ran through her recent successes in speaking up: yelling "Manitoba tuck," asking Mrs. Barry for help, inviting Dunya and Skylar to their table, and today, talking back to Ryan. She was actually living up to what Dad had wanted for her. She felt like she was flying.

"I ordered pizza," Mom was saying, as Lily came back to earth. "Your favorite, Hobart, extra cheese."

"In the house!"

"I have to do a little more work," Mom said, heading into the kitchen. "Lily, will you make the salad, please?"

"Sure."

As Lily stood up, Skippy ran to the door, barking.

"I'll see who it is!" Hobart said, and followed Skippy. He opened the door, but no one was there. When he turned around, Skippy was settling into his spot on the couch.

"Skippy!" Lily said. "Sorry, Hobart. He always fakes that there's someone at the door so we'll get off the couch and he can sit there. I should've known."

Hobart laughed. "That's okay. I'm getting writer's cramp, anyway, so I'll play with Skippy."

After a few minutes in the kitchen, Lily didn't hear the sound of Skippy's nails scratching the wood or his body occasionally slamming into the wall from not being able to stop himself in time. Instead, she heard Hobart talking. She popped her head into the living room and saw Hobart sunk into the couch. Skippy, who probably weighed almost as much as Hobart did, was lying across his lap, looking up at him as Hobart read aloud from his curling book.

Lily stood frozen. It reminded her of Dad reading to Skippy. It calmed Skippy down. Sure enough, Skippy's eyes kept closing and his head kept sinking until he'd jerk himself awake again.

She heard Mom close the laptop and, moments later, felt Mom put her arms around her and rested her chin gently on top of Lily's head. They stood in the kitchen doorway watching Hobart. Lily knew what her mom was thinking even before she said it because Lily was thinking the same thing. "Dad would've loved Hobart."

Libro

S igh.

That was a happy sigh, by the way, due to Lily's progress on her Strive for Five.

It would be easy for the Imaginer to end the story here—on a high note of hope.

Excuse me? Easier isn't better? It's not like real life?

Well, no, I suppose it's not. But I will still make the argument—

Sigh. That was not a happy sigh because the Imaginer has turned off the light in the attic, and that accursed screen saver is about to shut me out.

Oh, crikey! It's not even dawn yet. The Imaginer has returned with a vengeance and an enormous mug of coffee. Let me just say I'm glad I'm not the keyboard because that device is getting hammered.

Chapter 16

H obart clutched a stack of notes. "Ready?"

Lily's heart was beating fast, but she nodded as she followed Hobart down the hallway, sticking notes on the walls, lockers, and classroom doors as kids turned to watch. Lily was shaking too much to look at their reactions. She was glad for Hobart's bravery.

"I told my dad about these notes and how it's teaching people interesting facts and the truth about immigrants."

"What did he say?"

"He laughed at me. And he called it brainwashing."

"What?"

He stopped putting up notes for a moment. "It's like the facts don't matter. He's decided what he believes and that's it."

Lily found herself, again, not knowing what to say. She couldn't understand Mr. Hall. He was so different from her dad. She wished Dad could've had a chance to talk with him.

When they reached homeroom, Hobart stuck a note on the outside of the door, then the inside, then on Miss Chase's desk and on the whiteboard where Miss Chase was writing. The one on the whiteboard read, *Algebra began in Babylon, which is modern-day Iraq!*

"That's true," she said with a smile, but the note on her desk made her smile wider. *It's awesome that you're teaching Skylar algebra! Keep up the good work!*

Lily heard her say thank you, but Hobart had moved on and was adding notes to the windows. It gave Lily the courage to put some on the walls. Even in their noisy class, some kids noticed and walked over to read the notes.

There were smiles and giggles, nods and "That's cool!" or "Awesome!" And sneers from Ryan.

"What's this? Littering?" Ryan snatched some of the notes, crumpled them up, and threw them on the floor.

"No," Zoey snapped, pointing at the notes he'd dropped, *"that's* littering. Duh."

"Okay, class," Miss Chase said, "let's settle down. And thank you for these notes. I think they're very nice."

Ryan made a falsetto imitation of her voice. "I think they're very nice."

Zoey rolled her eyes and muttered, "Grow up, Ryan."

At least he stayed quiet for the Pledge of Allegiance. Lily noticed that he always did. But after that, he passed Lily a sticky note that said *Kick Me* and hissed, "Put it on Ho-fart's back!" cracking up along with his buddies.

"What is it?" Hobart whispered.

Lily just shook her head and crumpled the note into a tiny wad.

Throughout math, Ryan slipped them notes: *Bullies are meanies . . . wah! Teacher's pet! Who cares where Africa is?* He also sneered comments like "Losers," "You should leave with the illegal aliens," and "No one likes your stupid notes."

Even in social studies, when he could get away with it, he hissed comments to Lily, like, "You have Ho-fart disease" and "No one cares about you or your loser friends."

Lily tried hard to ignore him and was relieved to get to her lunch table where she had, as Hobart said, her "team."

Mr. Hammer walked up to their table. "How do you like this cool birthday present from my wife?" He raised his eyebrows and held up a Black Panther lunch box.

"Whoa!" Hobart said. "That's awesome!"

Skylar grinned.

"I'm going to go show it to my friends over there," Mr. Hammer said, motioning toward Ryan's table and giving them a wink. "By the way, these notes I'm seeing all over the place—"

"That's us!" Hobart said. "It was Lily's idea. We want

everyone to learn more about Dunya, and all the new kids, and where they came from."

"Why am I not surprised? I figured it had to be this crew." Mr. Hammer's smile reached all the way up to his eyes, which were also smiling. "I'm proud of you."

They all stared after the Hammer as he loped over to Ryan's table.

"He is a good man," Dunya whispered.

"Mind if I join you boys?" Mr. Hammer said in a loud voice. "Thanks!" he said, without waiting for an invitation. He sat down and made a show of opening his lunch box.

Ryan sneered at it.

"What?" Mr. Hammer said, his face stunned. "You don't know about Black Panther? Didn't you see the movie? Wakanda forever! Do you even know what that means?"

The boys at the table nodded, all except Ryan, who rolled his eyes.

"Hey," the Hammer said, leaning closer to the boys, "how about that part where—" Lily couldn't hear after that, but she saw most of the boys around Mr. Hammer talking and nodding, then punching their fists in the air.

Ryan kept sneering, but the other boys didn't notice him. Lily felt herself smile.

"Hey, can I eat with you guys?" It was Zoey, her hair still spiked but now green. "I usually eat in the library, but it's closed for a faculty meeting today."

"Sure," Lily said as she and Dunya moved their lunches over so Zoey had space.

Zoey picked up one of the notes on the table and read it aloud. "'Instead of bullying someone, why don't you get to know them? You might make a new friend.'" She nodded. "Yup. So what made you decide to do these notes?"

Lily explained the *why* behind the notes campaign.

"Cool," Zoey said. "Okay if I write some?"

"Of course!" Hobart handed her a pad of bright green sticky notes that matched her hair.

Zoey pulled a glitter pen from her backpack and wrote, *What can you do to save the planet?* She looked up. "I think it's really nice you put thank-you notes on the janitor's bucket and closet door."

Lily and Hobart eyed each other. "We didn't do that," Lily said.

Hobart grinned. "It's catching on!"

Lily and Hobart slipped out of the cafeteria early to see what new notes had appeared. "I'll just say," Hobart explained, "that I had to get something from my locker."

When they rounded the corner, Lily was sure there were more notes on the walls and lockers than what they'd put out that morning.

Hobart pointed to a scrap of lined paper, attached to a locker by shoving the edge into a vent slat. "That's not one of ours."

Lily read it out loud. "'I like how you always say you're too full to finish your lunch so you can give it to Carlos.'"

"Aw," said Hobart, "that's nice."

There were some silly notes, like *Here's a question. Why is there such a thing as school, anyway? Do we need it? No!* or *Football is the best sport. Everything else sucks.* Mostly, though, they were kind or thoughtful.

As they neared Hobart's locker, he was still searching for new notes, which gave Lily a chance to snatch one off of his locker before he saw it. *Ho-fart is a liar!* She was sure it was from Ryan.

The chimes rang, and a flood of kids entered the hallway. A girl read one of their sticky notes on her locker, rolled her eyes, and dropped it on the floor. Lily watched as another girl picked it up, read it, and squinted up at the ceiling for a moment before nodding, putting it in her notebook, and continuing down the hall.

"Thanks, Lily," Hobart said, reading another sticky note he'd taken off his locker.

"What?"

"Thanks for the note about liking my bow ties. I'll still wear them on special occasions."

"I didn't write that note, Hobart."

He smirked and rolled his eyes. "Sure!"

"No, really. Let me see that." He showed her the pink note with flowers drawn in every corner. "That's not my handwriting."

Hobart looked at the note again. "You're right, it's not." He grinned. "Someone likes my bow ties!"

A boy at the locker on the other side of Hobart's handed him a note. "This was on my locker, but it has your name on it."

Lily felt her shoulders tense as Hobart started to read the note. "'Hobart, you're really smart. Also, I think you're cute.'" He smiled, and Lily did, too, feeling her shoulders relax.

Hobart's smile waned. He looked at Lily. "Wait . . . cute like a stuffed animal?"

"No! That means you're handsome. People say that about grown-up men, too."

Hobart smiled again. "Okay. I guess I'm cute!"

Lily watched Hobart walk down the hall—quickly, as usual, but also seemingly taller, or maybe he was just holding his head up higher. That, thought Lily, was a big part of what the notes campaign was all about.

Libro

Reader, I adore these notes! Brilliant! Sparkling! Inspired! You know how much I love words.

Except, of course, when someone like Ryan gets involved. Can't that sneeze-lurker be nice for even half a minute? Well, yes, I suppose he can. During the Pledge of Allegiance.

However, I am not impressed that he is quietly respectful for mere seconds per day as he stands and addresses the flag. I do admire the words in your Pledge of Allegiance. Words are the very essence of my being, and I am quite adept at recognizing the outstanding ones. However, even I will admit that words are only strings of letters. Is it enough to simply stand and say them reverently? Or do you have to actually do something to ensure this "liberty and justice for all"?

Hint: The answer is, actually do something.

To quote that phrase you humans use when something is mind-numbingly obvious: *just sayin'*.

Chapter 17

Hobart had discovered that Dunya lived a few blocks away from them and invited her to join them on their walk home. They had to pick up her seven-year-old brother, Farouk, at the elementary school. As they approached the school, Hobart asked Dunya, "So is your dad one of the guys who was a driver or translator for our soldiers?"

"Translator, yes. He is fluent in five languages."

Hobart stopped, his eyes wide. "No way!"

Dunya laughed. "It is true. That is why I study French. I know some Kurdish. And Arabic, of course."

"And English," Lily added.

Dunya shook her head. "Only a little."

"Nuh-uh," Hobart said, "a *lot*!"

"Now my father paints."

"He's an artist, too?" Hobart said.

"He paints houses," Dunya explained, "and helps my mother to clean houses."

Lily always felt for immigrants who, even if they spoke English, seemed to have a hard time finding a job anything like what they had before.

Hobart frowned. "That must be weird when he's used to being a translator."

"It is fine. We are grateful to be here. It is only hard because we have no car so they can only work at places they can walk to."

Lily and Hobart shared a look. They were all quiet until reaching the elementary school.

Farouk took an instant liking to Hobart as they dribbled a soccer ball down the sidewalk. Hobart kept missing the ball, either accidentally or on purpose, and saying goofy things like, "Where did you get this googly ball? Did you put grease on it to make it slide?"

"You're like Adnan," Farouk said, giggling.

"Adnan is our cousin," Dunya explained. "He is very funny."

"Try stop this!" Farouk kicked the ball past Hobart and into the street, where a car braked hard and swerved.

Dunya yelled at Farouk, but not in English.

When the street was clear, Hobart retrieved the ball and handed it to Farouk, who dropped it on the sidewalk and put one foot on top of it.

Dunya continued reprimanding her brother, who rolled his eyes but then looked up at her with a grin. "I don't understand Arabic. You have to speak English."

Dunya gave him her mom stare. "Pick. Up. The. Ball. Did you understand that?"

"Hobart was playing, too," Farouk muttered as he picked up the soccer ball.

"Sorry," Hobart said quickly, "I'm not used to having a little brother."

Farouk looked up at him. "You have a sister?"

"Nope. Just me."

"I miss all my cousins," Farouk said. "It's like lots of brothers and sisters."

Dunya's voice was soft and kind. "You are making a lot of friends."

Farouk looked at the ground. "It's not the same."

"No, but we make it the best."

Farouk looked at her and his sad face grew a smile. "Make the best of it. Not *make it the best*! I'm smarter than you and I'm only seven!"

He ran ahead and Hobart followed closely after.

Dunya shrugged. "He is like my father, good with languages."

"So are you, Dunya. Seriously." She paused. "Do you miss your cousins, too?"

"Yes. But I am happy." She was smiling, but Lily couldn't help but feel that Dunya was trying to follow the advice she'd given her brother, to make the best of it.

Hobart and Farouk were already kicking the soccer ball in Lily's yard, and Skippy was jumping at the door doing his rooster bark.

"Coming!" Lily said, taking out her key.

Dunya was trying to latch the gate without success.

"It's okay," Lily said, "you can leave it."

"But the dog—"

"He won't get out because we're here."

Skippy tried to join in the soccer game, which made Farouk laugh. He laughed even more when Hobart fell and rolled in the grass, then popped up again, so Hobart kept doing it. Farouk was giggling uncontrollably when a voice boomed.

"What's going on here?"

Lily turned to see Mr. Hall, roughly pushing the gate open and stalking toward Hobart. He frowned at Dunya and Farouk, then turned to Hobart, hands on his waist. "Who are these kids?"

Hobart looked at the ground. "Dunya and Farouk."

"What?"

Hobart answered even more softly.

"Speak up!"

Dunya stepped toward Farouk and reached for his hand.

"I am Dunya," she said, her voice a little wobbly, but her head held high. "My brother, Farouk."

Mr. Hall exhaled sharply and didn't look at her but spoke loudly. "It's *My brother* is *Farouk.* You should learn English."

Dunya shrank before Lily's eyes, her head dropping and her shoulders slouching down and inward.

Lily's whole body tensed to the point she was shaking. She was relieved to see her mom pulling up to the sidewalk.

Mr. Hall turned to Lily. "Your mother wasn't here?"

Mom hurried through the open gate. "What's happening?"

"That's what I'd like to know," Mr. Hall said. He surveyed the yard. "I'm driving past and there's all these kids in your yard. They shouldn't be here on their own."

"That's true," Lily's mom said. "Lily and I will be talking about that."

"I'll be talking with Hobart, too." He narrowed his eyes at his son. "Get in the truck," he hissed.

Hobart, head down, slowly walked out the gate.

Lily saw her mom's mouth open, but no words came out. Lily wasn't sure where to be: comforting Dunya or supporting Hobart.

Mom introduced herself to Dunya and Farouk and started asking them questions about their schools and if

they wanted a snack.

As Mr. Hall headed for the truck, Lily heard him mutter, "Can't even speak English right."

Hobart paused, his hand clutching the gate handle, as he watched his father walk around the front of the truck. "How many languages do *you* speak?"

Mr. Hall froze and turned to Hobart. "What did you say?"

"Nothing," Hobart muttered, getting in the truck and sinking down in his seat.

Lily stared at the truck for a moment as it lurched away from the curb, then hurried over to Dunya.

"Are you sure you don't want to come in for a snack?" Mom was saying.

Dunya shook her head. "We need to go home."

"I can give you a ride."

"Thank you, but we will walk."

Mom gave Dunya her business card. "If *anyone*"—her eyes flitted in the direction of Hobart's house—"gives your family any trouble, have your parents call me."

Lily walked them to the gate. "I'm really sorry. Hobart's not like that at all. It's just his dad."

Dunya nodded distractedly, pushing Farouk ahead of her.

"See you Monday," Lily said as she watched them hurry away.

Once inside, Lily told her mom what happened. "Mr. Hall was just mad that Hobart was playing with immigrant kids!"

Her mother grimaced. "I suspected that."

"Then why didn't you say something? You shouldn't let him get away with being racist. You were being too polite!"

"I didn't hear anything he said except that you kids shouldn't be here on your own, and he's right about that."

"We were just hanging out together. Why is that a problem?"

"I'm a lawyer, Lily. I can't help but see everything as a problem." She sighed and sat down at the kitchen table. "If someone gets hurt, I've given implied consent for everyone to be in my yard, and I'm liable for any injuries or anything that goes wrong."

"Nothing's going to go wrong!"

"You never know," Mom said. "Look. When I'm here, you're welcome to have friends over. In the meantime, maybe Dunya and Farouk would like to join you in the park when you take Skippy. That's a public place. Everyone is welcome," she added with a frown. "Last time I checked."

Lily worried about Hobart but didn't want to call or visit because she didn't want to get Hobart in more trouble. His dad obviously wasn't happy with her. Well, she wasn't particularly happy with him.

She wasn't happy with her mom, either, and Mom knew it. She tried to talk with Lily at dinner that night.

"Lily, you know I'm supportive of immigrants, and I'm sorry Mr. Hall behaved—"

"He had no right to scare them like that, or be so mean to Hobart!"

"You're right. But I can't fight every battle, especially when I wasn't—"

"Dad said you start by making changes locally. In your own neighborhood. Like with Mr. Hall. That's how you make the world a better place!"

Mom nodded but didn't say anything. By the tears in Mom's eyes, Lily knew it was because she'd brought up Dad. They both missed him terribly. She swallowed hard, regretting having lashed out.

"Sorry, Mom," she whispered.

Her mother reached across the table and squeezed Lily's hand, giving her a forced smile.

On Saturday, Skippy sprawled on the rug in Lily's room as she looked through her many photo albums, starting from when she was a baby. Mom had made her get rid of most of her old projects she'd done with Dad because they didn't have room in their new house. "And anyway," Mom had said, "you have pictures." Lily felt a lump in her throat as she looked through the albums, wishing she still had the actual items, even though most of them were falling apart, like the baking soda and vinegar volcano and the popsicle-stick trebuchet.

When she got to the picture of the huge map she and Dad had made that covered half the basement of their old house, she felt a twinge of guilt. It was for GeoBee, even though she hadn't officially participated in the event. It was their own private GeoBee.

Lily put down her tablet, went to the closet, and pulled out the large box painted with the continents. Skippy looked up for a moment, then put his head down again, seeing she wasn't going for her bedroom door. Mom had let her keep her GeoBee items because she knew they were too important to Lily and her dad. Among the 3D models of various countries, the pop-up cards of iconic buildings, and the homemade mancala board, she saw her geography journal. It recorded the dates of her accomplishments. Lily smiled at her dad's entries: *Lily learned all the capitals in Africa! Lily learned all the flags of Asia! Lily can explain global warming!*

She lost her smile, though, when she saw *Lily participated in GeoBee!* The date column for that entry was empty.

She closed the journal and hurriedly repacked the box, pushing it into her closet.

Sighing, Lily pulled out the letter from her dad and read it once again, wondering if she would ever stop missing him. She shook her head. "No."

Skippy startled, staring at her.

"I wasn't talking to you, Skippy. Do you want to play?"

Skippy scrambled to his feet and waited by her bedroom door expectantly.

Outside, as she threw balls for Skippy, she was still thinking about Dad, and wondered what was happening between Hobart and his dad. Whatever it was, she was sure it wasn't good.

Libro

*C*rikey! Hobart's father makes me feel like blowing the electrons out of this computer!

Where to begin?

On a minor point, I will say that the Imaginer is, indeed, a lawyer. So, yes, she does see potential peril in everything. Which is also a trait in Imaginers. She is hit doubly hard. It's a wonder she manages to get up every day and carry on. Hence, the copious cups of coffee.

On a major point . . . Mr. Hall. I take back even what I said about Mr. Hall being generous because, really, I was being generous saying that.

I understand he is upset about his friend who was killed in Afghanistan, but why is he taking his anger out on children—who are from Iraq, incidentally, which is a different country from Afghanistan. (Perhaps Mr. Hall needs to be in GeoBee.) Honestly, if he read the information Hobart printed out for him about immigrants, he would see that they are people just like him.

News flash: You are all the same species! Why do you turn on your own?

Chapter 18

On their way to school Monday morning, Lily wanted to ask Hobart what happened with his dad, but Hobart never gave her a chance to get a word in.

"You know that curling book I read? I was thinking, it's great and all, but they should totally make a curling book for kids, and then I thought, hey, maybe I should write it? Do you think I should write a book?" He didn't pause long enough for Lily to answer. "I'm getting a lot of practice writing all those notes, right? I wrote more over the weekend. Did you? This is my favorite: *Can you list at least ten dog breeds that have a geographic location in their name?* Spoiler alert, there's way more than ten! You can get ten just by listing terrier breeds. So, anyway, if I added up all the notes I've written, I've probably written a book! Okay, at least a chapter."

Lily knew he didn't want to talk about his dad's behavior, but by the time they reached homeroom and he was finally winding down, she couldn't help asking.

"What happened after you and your dad left my house on Friday?"

Hobart shrugged. "He just yelled at me."

"What did he say?"

"That I shouldn't be seen with outsiders because I'm already weird enough."

"I'm sorry," Lily mumbled.

"My dad says stuff like that, too."

Lily and Hobart spun around to see Skylar standing there, holding Hobart's curling book.

"I—I'm just returning this. You're right. It really is like chess on ice."

Hobart took the book and eyed Skylar. "Your dad says stuff like that about immigrants?"

"No. About me."

"You're not weird," Hobart said.

Skylar shrugged. "My mom says he's stressed. Did your dad job lose his job?"

"No." Hobart glanced at Lily before asking, "Did yours?"

Skylar looked away. "Maybe."

Hobart thought for a moment. "Hey, when I was in second grade and my dad wasn't working, I got free lunch."

Skylar shook his head. "He doesn't want anyone to know.

We have to take care of ourselves. I just have to buck up and be a man."

"But you're a kid!" Hobart said.

"Yeah, but I don't have to be a spoiled brat."

Lily felt her jaw drop. "Is that what your dad says?" She couldn't imagine Skylar ever acting spoiled or bratty.

Hobart clenched his fists. "He shouldn't say that."

"It's okay," Skylar said. "If I just stay quiet, he doesn't bother me."

The chimes sounded for the beginning of math and Skylar darted back to his seat.

Hobart turned to Lily, his nostrils flaring, and hissed, "His dad shouldn't say stuff like that to him! It's not true! And it's not fair!"

"No," Lily said, "it isn't." And she meant Hobart's dad, too.

As she watched Hobart sit down heavily, elbows on the desk, forehead on his balled fists, she was pretty sure he was talking about his dad, too.

After math, Lily decided to walk Hobart to his locker. She noticed more notes had cropped up. Some of them were thoughtful but others, well, it felt to Lily like Mr. Hall had written them. And they were typed so there was no handwriting to give a clue about who wrote them. Lily had her suspicions.

The notes said things like Ryan would say: *Go home!*

You have your own home! Stop coming here! No illegal aliens welcome!

It reminded Lily of the time she and Dad were walking to their Prius in the library parking lot after he'd been teaching. They saw a guy yelling, "Go home!" at the two women, who were Dad's students, as they got in their car. Dad had walked over to the man in the cap and T-shirt, Lily following, even though Dad had told her to stay put.

She was surprised at how calm Dad's voice had been, and she'd never forget what he said. "They've earned their right to be here. Have you?"

The man had been flustered. "I—I was born here!"

"A feat accomplished by your mother," Dad had pointed out. "Have *you* done anything to earn this privilege?"

The man then started calling Dad names and swearing, and Dad had quickly ushered her to the car, telling her to ignore him.

She wished Dad were here now to tackle this ugly problem.

"Come *on*, Lily!" Hobart was whipping the nasty notes off lockers, doors, and walls. "Help me, before everyone sees these!"

It woke Lily from her memory, and she helped pull down the notes, including the ones on Hobart's locker that said *Ho-fart.*

It was worse at lunch. And Mr. Hammer wasn't even

there because he was chaperoning a field trip. Ryan carried his tray past their table, leaned in toward Dunya, and said, "Go back to your country."

Hobart stood up and shouted, "Hey! Don't say that! This *is* her country!"

A long tone sounded over the PA system. "This is Principal Cooper. It has come to my attention that there have been . . . unfortunate notes posted around the school. I understand there were some positive notes to begin with, but from now on, with the exception of *appropriate* campaign posters, there will be no notes permitted on lockers, walls, or anywhere else."

"It's like when one kid acts out and the teacher bans recess for everyone," Zoey said, crossing her arms and shaking her head.

"It's not fair!" Hobart said, echoing exactly what Lily was thinking.

Dunya was looking across the cafeteria. "What is everyone doing over there?"

They turned to see Ryan writing his name on the student council candidate sign-up sheet by the cafeteria door. Brady was putting up campaign posters.

Hobart groaned. "Oh, great. Ryan is running for student council president! I think I'm going to throw up."

They read the posters Brady taped on the wall about what Ryan would do, each one with a separate promise in huge letters: No Homework! Cell Phones Allowed in Class! Free Ice Cream on Fridays. Choose Your Own Schedule!

"He can't do any of those things!" Hobart said.

Even as he said it, students were cheering, some of them even chanting, "Ry-an! Ry-an! Ry-an! Ry-an!"

Lily felt her stomach turn sour. "I can't believe it," she whispered.

"Believe it," Zoey said through gritted teeth.

Hobart put his head on the table.

A group of giggling girls surrounded Ryan as he headed back to his table. "Can you really do all that?" one of the girls asked.

"Of course," Ryan said. "How do you think those stupid notes got banned? I just did that. My parents have connections on the school board. Pretty soon I'm going to get some pathetic teachers fired. I'm in control here. No one else even needs to bother running."

Samantha and Ava, wearing the same expensive-looking clothes, sauntered up to Ryan's table. Samantha asked, "Is it true you're going to start a dress code?"

Brady looked down at his plaid shirt, then stared at Ryan. "What, like uniforms?"

"Of course not, moron," Ryan said. "Designer clothes or at least something that's in fashion." He looked over pointedly at Lily's table.

The girls smirked as they walked past Skylar, rolling

their eyes.

Skylar swallowed and put his sandwich down, dropping his head to look at his wrinkled T-shirt.

"Hey," Zoey said, "don't worry about it, Skylar. They're laughing at my shorants."

"What are 'shorants'?'" Dunya asks.

"Yeah," said Hobart, "what are 'shorants'?'"

Zoey stood up so they could see her better. "These are what I call shorants. Shorts over pants!" She sat down and shrugged. "I like creating my own outfits. I only shop at Goodwill and Salvation Army. Bonus: It's recycling."

Lily marveled at Zoey's independence. And bravery. And how she stuck up for Skylar.

When Samantha and Ava walked past with their trays again, Zoey said, "Hi, twins! Wow, really original to buy the exact same outfits." Their smug smiles faltered. Zoey smiled, batting her eyelids. "You must be so proud of your . . . creativity." The girls walked hurriedly away.

"Whoa," Hobart said, "I'm glad you're on our team, Zoey. You can be scary!"

"I know, but once in a while people like that need a wake-up call."

"Hey, everyone!" Ryan yelled. "Free ice cream! Compliments of me!"

Lily looked over to see Ryan's mom pushing a dolly of boxes of ice-cream sandwiches.

"Aw, man," Hobart said with a sigh.

Lily shook her head.

"Is it really free ice cream?" a small girl in pigtails asked.

"No," Zoey barked, "it's not free at all!"

The girl stepped back.

"She means," Lily said quickly, "that Ryan is trying to bribe people to vote for him by giving them ice cream, so it's not exactly free."

The girl's jaw dropped as she turned to Ryan's table. "Ew! Then I don't want it!" She looked back at Lily, her hands on her hips. "That's not the way it's supposed to work."

"No," said Lily, "it's not."

Libro

People, people, people. How can so many believe Ryan and his lies and false promises? Honestly, as individuals, I find you humans to be quite thoughtful, kind, wise, and considerate, but something seems to happen when you become part of a group that starts mindless chanting. It is as if you have only one brain among you and, unfortunately, it does not appear to be the brightest one. Yet people will follow it without thinking.

Sheep follow each other for no good reason, too. I have seen a video the Imaginer took of sheep in a beautiful grassy field. One of them decided to jump over a low stone wall into a rather rocky and less grassy field, and the other sheep felt compelled to follow. When they arrived, they all looked around blinking, as if to say, *What on earth am*

I doing here? And how did I get here? And how do I get back?

Sheep look decidedly ridiculous standing together in a field, eyes blinking and tongues lolling to one side. Crikey! Reader, don't be a sheep!

Chapter 19

The next day, as Lily, Hobart, and Dunya were leaving school for their walk home, Ryan blocked their way. "Goodbye, *Dumb*-ya," he said slowly, "and I mean goodbye. I'm getting all the aliens kicked out of our school and sent to a different district." He smirked and pushed past them, adding, "Until you get sent back to where you came from!"

Hobart clenched his fists. "Hey!"

"No," Dunya said, "ignore him. Do not let him know he bothers you."

Lily agreed with Dunya, but she felt angry and frustrated like Hobart.

"I am happy Farouk isn't here," Dunya said. "It is not fair for a little boy to hear this."

"It's not fair for anyone!" Hobart said, kicking stones out of his path.

"Why do people hate us so much?" Dunya said quietly.

Hobart swallowed hard and looked away.

They picked up Farouk and took Skippy to the park, but Hobart's soccer playing was half-hearted. Even Skippy didn't make Hobart laugh.

"Come on!" Farouk said, heading the ball to Hobart. "Do one of your funny kicks!"

Hobart returned the ball, but Farouk stopped it with his foot and put his hands on his hips. "Dude! That wasn't funny!"

"Farouk!" Dunya called. "Don't be rude." She shook her head at Lily, who smiled back.

"Do the one where you fall down. Like this!" Farouk demonstrated an exaggerated fall, spinning in circles before doing a face-plant near the park gate and giggling.

Skippy jumped over him and ran to Hobart, as if wanting to be part of the game.

Suddenly, Farouk stopped laughing and stood up, grabbing his ball against his chest. "He's here," he said, looking at Hobart.

"Hobart!"

The others turned to see what Farouk had already noticed: Hobart's dad.

"What?" Hobart said. "We're not at Lily's house."

Hobart's tone wasn't exactly defiant, Lily noticed, but it also wasn't weak.

"It's time to come home," Mr. Hall said, glaring at his son, and then at Lily. "We've talked about this. I thought you understood."

Hobart looked away, breathing heavily, then pressed his lips together and walked to the park gate. Lily half thought he was going to talk to his dad, maybe tell him he was going to stay at the park, but instead he slammed the gate closed behind him and marched over to the truck. He yanked the door open and sat down heavily.

Lily startled when Hobart slammed his door so hard the entire truck wobbled.

"What happened?" Lily asked Hobart when he joined her the next morning for the walk to school. This time she wasn't going to let him avoid talking about it.

"Well," Hobart said, "when I got in the truck yesterday, before my dad had a chance to start yelling at me, I yelled at him."

"You did?" Lily felt her eyes widen.

He looked at the ground as they walked. "Yeah. I said, 'I thought you supported our troops, like Melissa!' He said of course he supports our troops. Then I said, 'Well, so did Dunya's family from Iraq!' and I told him how her dad was a translator for our soldiers and was in danger every day, and that's why her family is here now. I also said, 'That kind of makes them patriotic Americans, same as us, doesn't it?'" Hobart took a big breath and let out a sigh. "Except I didn't say it like a question. I was still kind of yelling."

"Was he mad?"

"He was trying to laugh it off, until we got home. That's when I gave him all the emails I printed out from the soldiers."

"Soldiers? What soldiers?"

Hobart took a deep breath and puffed out his cheeks, letting his breath out slowly. "You know how you said your dad interviewed people in local government who'd fought in Iraq and Afghanistan, and they supported immigration?"

Lily nodded.

"Well, my dad keeps saying letting immigrants into our country is unpatriotic because it's disrespectful to soldiers, as if soldiers must hate immigration. But like my mom said, that's not the way Melissa feels. So, I emailed Melissa, and she said she'd ask soldiers in her unit if they'd answer my question, and a lot of them did, even her boss. And guess what?"

"What?"

"They all said they support the people who want to come here. Do you know that some soldiers lost their friends, too? And they still support immigration? They said it's good, caring, hardworking people who want to come here. They also said, if you had a chance to escape a horrible situation, even possible death, wouldn't you want to save your family? I printed them out and gave them to my dad."

"What did he say?"

Hobart moved his shoulders in something between a shrug and a cringe. "I kind of just shoved them at him. Then I told him Dunya's parents are cleaning houses and can't even get many cleaning jobs because they don't have a car, and how would he like it if that happened to him. Then I went in my room and slammed my door."

"That was brave, Hobart. You did the right thing."

"I don't know. My parents went in their room and slammed *their* door and my mom was yelling, which she normally never does, and my dad was yelling, which isn't unusual, and this morning he was sleeping on the sofa. My mom was still mad—not at me, I don't think, but she was kind of, you know . . ."

"Snippy?"

"Yeah."

"My mom gets like that sometimes, too."

Hobart nodded. "At least I made friends with some more soldiers."

"Are you going to keep emailing them?"

"Maybe Sergeant Major Timothy Johnson. He's Melissa's boss, and he said he was really impressed that a kid would be trying to figure this out."

They'd almost reached the front of the school, but Hobart stopped. He hesitated a moment and pulled a folded piece of paper out of his back pocket. He opened it up and slowly held it out to Lily without looking at her.

It was a string of emails from "SGT MAJ Timothy Johnson," but the one at the top, the most recent, said, "Hobart, you're ten years old and already wiser than a lot of grown-ups I know. I have a little boy and I hope he's as smart as you when he's ten. I bet your daddy is real proud of you."

Lily nodded. "He's right. What did your dad say?"

"I didn't show him this one."

"Why not?" Of all the emails, Lily thought, this was the one his father needed to see.

Hobart shrugged. "I didn't want him to laugh." He took the paper, refolded it, and returned it to his pocket.

Lily felt an ache in her throat. "Hobart?"

He looked over at her.

"My dad would've been proud of you," she whispered.

"Thanks," Hobart whispered back.

Libro

I do love it when you humans take matters into your own hands. The Imaginer calls it "character arc." I call it "How about that Hobart?" He stood up to his father and caused quite a kizzle kazzle.[2]

Hobart is simply trying to get to the truth. And why not? Why choose ignorance when the information is out there? So many smart words to read! Also, unlike myself, you have the ability to talk with other people and make some new friends, so go enjoy.

I won't be jealous.

Much.

---

2 *Kizzle kazzle* is a curling term referring to a stone that is purposely shot down the ice in a wobbly manner, for some reason. I don't particularly care about the purpose, I simply like the sound of the term *kizzle kazzle*, which even feels wobbly.

Chapter 20

*L*unch that day was a double period to allow for student council campaigning. Hobart was quiet, which made the commotion at Ryan's table all the more noticeable.

"What's going on?" Skylar asked.

Zoey plunked her tray down with an exasperated sigh. "More bribes."

Ryan was handing out free swag like at the college football games Lily used to go to with her parents. He had keychains with flashlights, full-sized candy bars, and foam footballs, all with Vote Ryan on them.

Lily felt her eyes narrowing as she looked at Ryan's table and the students happily grabbing things.

"Other people need to run for president," Dunya said.

"Yeah," Zoey said, "especially since Ryan is telling

people not to run. I don't want him to get away with that."

Lily sighed. "It wouldn't make any difference, anyway. Look how happy everyone is with all the toys and candy they're getting from Ryan."

"But that is not what is important," Dunya said. "It is people. And ideas."

"That's what's *supposed* to matter," Hobart mumbled.

Dunya tilted her head toward Lily and paused for a moment. "Lily, you have ideas."

"She's right," Hobart said, turning to look at Lily like he was just waking up. "You do!"

Zoey and Skylar nodded their agreement.

Lily stared at them. "Oh, no. No. I could never run for student council."

"Why not?" Mr. Hammer said, sitting down between Hobart and Skylar with his Black Panther lunch box. "The candidate sign-up sheet is right over there," he said, giving a nod toward the cafeteria door.

Lily was too tongue-tied to answer. There were so many reasons why. She wouldn't be any good at it. She wasn't a leader. She wasn't interested in local government. She couldn't talk in front of people. Nobody even knew her.

"She's shy," Hobart said.

"Then why don't you, Hobart?" the Hammer asked him.

He shrugged. "We're kind of the nerdy kids, not the popular ones."

"Which means you're like ninety-five percent of the students," the Hammer replied.

"True," Zoey agreed. "Maybe you *should* run, Hobart."

"Or you," he said.

"Nah, I'm a little too weird for most people's taste. You're a normal kid."

"Hardly," Hobart muttered.

"I'd vote for you," Skylar said.

"Me, too," Lily added.

Dunya smiled. "Yes, and we will all help you."

"Come on," Mr. Hammer said. "Go for it."

Hobart gave a long sigh but then shrugged and stood up. "Okay. Why not? Lily, you sure you don't want to be president?"

"I'm positive." And she was. Almost entirely. A tiny part of her wished that she'd try running for student council, because she knew Dad would've challenged her to, but she was relieved Hobart was the one running.

When an apple hit the floor by their table, Mr. Hammer picked it up and strode over to the corner of the cafeteria. Lily was impressed he knew where the apple had come from. As she watched him, she noticed Hobart signing his name on the student council candidate sheet.

After Mr. Hammer marched several boys out of the cafeteria, Ryan's ugly laughter reached their table. "No one would vote for you, Ho-fart. And you don't even have a platform. You're just running around saying"—Ryan raised his voice an octave—"'Vote for me, vote for me!'" He shook his head. "Get real!"

Hobart rejoined them at the table. "Okay, never mind."

"Ryan's right," Lily said.

Dunya shook her head vigorously. "No!"

"I mean, the 'Get real' part."

Zoey stared at her. "Are you serious?"

Skylar was staring at her, too, and Hobart hung his head.

"I mean, *Get REAL* can be our slogan and our platform!"

"I don't get it," Hobart said.

"Look." She grabbed her notebook and a pen. Skylar took out his pencil and chewed on it as Lily wrote.

Get
R
E
A
L

"The letters *R-E-A-L* stand for the pillars of our platform." Lily thought about her mom—"Get *Responsible* for your *Education*." She filled in the *R* with *Responsible* and the *E* with *Education*.

"What does this mean, exactly?" Dunya asked.

"Well, students in my homeroom, at least, are acting pretty irresponsibly—they don't treat the books and tablets, or even the teacher, very nicely."

"No kidding," Zoey said.

"My dad used to say, 'Walk the Talk,'" Lily said. She saw Dunya's blank look. "It means to actually do what you say, not just say the words."

"Hey!" Hobart said. "*A* could stand for *Actions*, like not throwing food in the cafeteria, and not saying mean things about immigrants." He paused for a moment, frowning. "Because if you really support our troops, you should listen to what they say."

Lily knew he was thinking about his dad. "That's good, Hobart," she said, and wrote *Actions*. "What should *L* be?"

"It should be something bigger than education and actions," Zoey said.

"Life," Skylar said, his face serious.

"Perfect!" Lily finished filling in their Get REAL platform and held it up for the others to see.

"Cool!" Hobart said, as Skylar nodded.

Zoey shook her head. "Ryan's posters say specific things he's going to do"—she held up her hands as the others started talking at once—"I'm not saying he can do any of them, but we should have a list of what we're offering. What could we do?"

Hobart shook his head. "Compared to Ryan and all his money? Not much."

"Well," Zoey said, "what doesn't cost anything?"

"Longer lunch," Skylar said.

They all looked at him.

"Seriously?" Zoey said. "You hardly even eat."

Skylar shrugged. "I just want free time. I could do math. Or puzzle books. Or play chess if anyone had a chess set." He looked up, hopefully.

"That's it!" Hobart pumped his fists. "Skippy breaks!"

"What are Skippy breaks?" Dunya asked.

Hobart grinned. "Tell them, Lily!"

"Well, when I was homeschooled, we played with my dog for a break. We don't have dogs, but if we had a longer lunch, there'd be time for kids to go outside or play games inside—"

"Or do art," Zoey added.

"But how is it possible to have more lunch?" Dunya said.

"Make lunch thirty-five and a half minutes instead of twenty," Skylar said softly. They all looked at him and he cleared his throat, twirling his pencil in his hands. "If we took off eight of the fifteen minutes from homeroom, and two and half minutes from the switching time between classes—because we really don't need five minutes—that's an extra fifteen and a half minutes."

"See?" Hobart said. "I knew you were a math genius!"

Zoey stood up and raised her arms in victory. "Yes! I'm

going to talk to the teachers and Mrs. Cooper. Miss Chase definitely doesn't need fifteen minutes at the start of each day for people to act out." When she sat down, though, her face clouded over. "Wait. If we have a lot of activities, we need teachers to lead them all, and there may not be enough teachers with free periods."

"Volunteers!" Hobart said. "Like Mr. Hammer. My mom would volunteer. She can teach calligraphy so we could all write like Dunya!"

Dunya smiled. "My grandmother would love to teach cooking or talk about life in Iraq."

"That would be so interesting," Lily said, "and helpful."

"Where would we have all these activities?" Zoey asked.

"Well," Lily said, "we could start by using tables in the cafeteria. Remember how the welcome table was along the side of the wall? We could have a bunch of tables against the wall."

"Maybe we could have snacks?" Skylar said.

Hobart grinned. "Definitely! You like my mom's brownies, right?"

Skylar's eyes widened as he nodded.

"Skylar," Zoey said, "my dad would totally love having someone to play chess with. And so would I, because I hate chess, and he's always trying to get me to play!"

"Awesome," Skylar whispered.

Hobart turned to Lily and spoke softly. "I wish your dad were here. He could teach kids how to do an interview, or how to write . . . or how not to be against immigrants."

"Me, too," Lily said quietly. Dad could teach anything and make it fun.

Zoey held up the piece of paper she'd been writing on.

Get
Recess
Electives
Art
Lunch

"Now that's a slogan I can get behind!" Hobart said.

"Good," said Lily, "because if you're going to be president, you need to know your platform!"

He looked at Lily. "Okay, I'll do it, but on one condition: you have to be vice president."

Lily's stomach churned. She couldn't speak, but simply shook her head.

"What does vice president do?" Dunya asked.

Skylar shrugged. "Help, but in the background. The president is the one out front."

He was right, especially with Hobart, who would do all the talking. It made Lily feel a lot better. Being a silent partner wouldn't be too bad. "Okay," she finally breathed.

"Hey, Skylar!" Hobart said. "You should be treasurer! You're already doing algebra!"

Skylar stared at him for a moment but then nodded.

Hobart looked at Dunya and Zoey. "Does one of you want to be secretary?"

"Not me!" Zoey said.

"What does secretary do?" Dunya asked.

"Writes down notes about meetings," Zoey said, "and maybe writes a newsletter."

"I will do that," Dunya said. "My tutor will help me. She wants me to do a writing project. I want to do this one."

"Well," Zoey said, "you know what you guys are missing, right?"

The others looked at each other, unsure.

"A campaign manager! Duh! You've got to get your information out there and drum up support. I'll do that. Unlike the rest of you, except maybe Hobart, I'm not exactly shy." She stood up and grabbed her tray. "I'm going to the art room right now to make up some campaign signs! Mrs. Oh lets me use the backs of old posters."

"Can I help?" Dunya said.

"We can all help," Lily said, and Skylar stood up, too.

"No," Zoey said, "you and Hobart have to stay here and campaign. Potential voters might want to talk to you."

Hopefully only to Hobart, Lily thought. Like Skylar said, a vice president helped in the background. Lily intended to stay way, *way* in the background.

* * *

Lily startled at the rapping on the kitchen door that evening. Skippy crowed his rooster bark, skidded to the door, and jumped up and down on his hind legs, pawing at the window.

"Who is that?" Mom said, looking up from her laptop.

"I can't see," Lily said. "Skippy! Down!"

Mom got up to hold Skippy, so Lily could open the door.

It was Hobart, bouncing on his toes, but still managing to throw a ball into the far corner of the yard for Skippy.

"Hi, Hobart," Mom said.

"Guess what, guess what, guess what?"

"What?" Lily asked.

"My dad's finally buying a new pickup!"

"Oh." Lily found it hard to get excited about something like that, especially when she was thinking about how Mr. Hall treated Hobart.

Hobart was still bouncing. "Guess why, guess why!"

"Why?"

"Because he's giving our truck to Dunya's family!"

"What?" Lily and her mom said at the same time.

Lily stared at Hobart while that sank in.

Skippy dropped the ball at their feet and Lily slowly picked it up, tossed it for him, and turned back to Hobart. "How did that happen?"

"Remember that email I showed you that I didn't show my dad?"

Lily nodded.

"Well, today my dad read all the emails on the computer. He was looking to see if there were any from soldiers who said they didn't want immigrants here. That's when he saw the one from Sergeant Major Timothy Johnson. Mom said he froze and read it again. Then he read it over and over and kept clearing his throat, which is what he does when he's nervous. So, apparently, he and my mom had a 'heart to heart'—that's what my mom called it. And at dinner tonight, he said that since Dunya's dad directly helped our soldiers, he should get our old truck."

"Wow," Lily said.

"I know!" Hobart took a deep breath and grinned. "And he said something he's never said before, or maybe"— Hobart scrunched up his face thinking—"never *not* said before."

"What?"

Hobart lowered his voice to sound more like his dad. "'I never said I wasn't proud of you.' And then, before he went to help Melissa's mom with some plumbing problem, he rubbed my head and did kind of a hug thing. My mom said it was a big step for him, but I already knew that."

Mom threw her head back and smiled. "I'm so happy for you, Hobart!"

Lily grinned, giving Hobart a hug. "That is awesome!"

Libro

*Y*es, all right, fine. I will go back, once again, to calling Mr. Hall generous. Honestly, it is so much harder to write someone off completely if they have a good quality or two. Why does the Imaginer do that? More importantly, he actually listed to Hobart! Huzzah, Hobart!

And how about that Lily? Coming up with Get REAL! And agreeing to be vice president? That is stepping out of one's comfort zone even if she intends "to stay way, way in the background." As Mrs. Barry says, "Impressive!"

Chapter 21

On their way to school the next morning, Lily could feel herself smiling. "It's great how your dad is turning around."

"Well, not completely. He said he can accept immigrants, but it doesn't mean he has to be friends with them."

"He might change."

Hobart gave her a sideways glance. "You think so?"

"It's possible. If he gets to know some immigrants."

"True," Hobart said. "Because if he gets to know them, then it's harder to hate them, right?" He gave a small smile. "Maybe some immigrants like hockey."

At lunch, Lily's group watched as Zoey unrolled eye-catching Get REAL posters with their slate of candidates. "Zoey! These are fantastic!"

Zoey shrugged but Lily saw she was smiling. "I made them this morning."

Skylar stood up to see the posters better. "I like how you have the tear-off slips at the bottom."

Lily hadn't even noticed that feature yet because of all the glitter and pompoms.

Dunya turned her head to read the tear-off sections. "Ah. It says the different things Get REAL means. That is a very good idea."

"Listen, team," Zoey said, "we need to decide who's giving speeches. Usually, the president does, and sometimes the vice president, and they both sit at the front of the room."

Lily groaned inside. Sitting up front with everyone staring at her would be bad enough, but standing up and speaking? In front of the school? She was *not* going to do that.

"Sometimes," Zoey went on, "the secretary or treasurer goes up for a short speech, kind of like a warm-up act to introduce the president, before returning to their table."

Dunya's eyes widened and Skylar shook his head.

Zoey crossed her arms. "Skylar, it's important for you to speak because it shows the difference between Ryan's claims like free ice cream and pick your own classes, none of which are supported by any facts, and our campaign promises, which we can keep."

"That's true," Lily said. "You have actual facts—the

number of minutes lunch would be and where, exactly, those minutes come from. Zoey, have you had a chance to find out about cutting down the time in homeroom and between classes?"

"Yup! Mrs. Cooper likes the idea of less time for people to 'get rowdy' between classes and wants to try two and a half minutes. Apparently, the five minutes is to get us used to middle and high school, except those schools are way bigger than ours. Also, a lot of teachers say they don't need fifteen minutes for homeroom, and kids don't need a break at the beginning of the day—they need a longer lunch, so she's thinking about experimenting with that, too."

"But can't someone else give those statistics?" Skylar asked.

"If I stand up and talk about a newsletter," Dunya said, "will you stand up, too?"

Skylar hesitated. Lily figured he must be thinking the same thing she was—if Dunya could stand up and address a crowd in a different language, shouldn't I be brave enough?

Finally, Skylar nodded, adding, "Just the facts, that's all."

Zoey stood up. "Good, then it's settled. Let's go put these posters up. Lily and Hobart, you stay here and work the crowd."

Hobart dutifully went from table to table in the cafeteria

and "worked the crowd."

Lily sat at their table, desperately hoping no one would talk to her. She found herself looking over at Ryan's table to see what freebies he was handing out today—candy tins full of M&M's with Rs on them—and saw Ryan slap Brady's hand as he reached for one of the tins.

"Not for you, moron," Ryan barked. "You're already voting for me!"

Lily shook her head. And they were supposed to be friends?

Brady spun around, catching Lily shaking her head and staring at him.

Lily quickly looked away just as Hobart returned to their table. "That's at least thirty-seven votes so far!"

"That's great!" Lily said.

"Yup," Hobart agreed, then scrunched his nose. "Except that there are a hundred and nineteen sixth graders."

Lily started to answer, but Zoey marched up to the table, her face stern. Dunya and Skylar followed, their heads hanging. "Look at this." She held out a sheet of paper. "They're circulating around the cafeteria. I think it's from Ryan."

When Hobart read it, his eyes widened and his mouth dropped open.

Lily noticed a lot of kids in the cafeteria staring at their table, most of them giggling. She read the page, too. "What?" she breathed.

Hobart Hall is only ten and pees on the playground!

Zoey Boyd has a temper. Watch out. You never know what she might do.

Is Skylar Anderson's dad a thief? He might end up in jail!

Dunya is from Iraq. That's all you need to know.

"This is—this is—!" Hobart sputtered.

Ryan and his followers, except Brady, appeared at their table.

"You wrote this, didn't you?" Zoey demanded.

Ryan grinned wider.

"It's all lies!"

Ryan shrugged, barely able to contain his laughter. "Hey, it's the truth. Ask Hobart."

Hobart glared at him and asked darkly, "Where's Brady?"

Ryan ignored him, pointing at Dunya. "She *is* from Iraq."

Lily's voice was shaking but she made herself speak. "You make it sound like it's something bad, like there's something more to it."

"I'm only repeating stuff that everyone says."

"Oh, really," Zoey said, her jaw set. "Everyone says Skylar's dad is a thief?"

"That's just a question. Maybe he is, maybe he isn't. Who knows?"

"You're a deceitful liar!" Zoey said.

Ryan smirked. "See? Bad temper."

"Wait—you're lying?" Ava asked as she stopped with her tray.

"Of course not. Are you stupid enough to fall for what they're saying?"

"I'm not stupid, Ryan."

"Good, then you know I'm right."

Ava narrowed her eyes at him, turned, and strode off.

"Where is your evidence for any of this?" Zoey barked.

Ryan shrugged, still smirking, and they watched him and his followers saunter back to his table, where Brady sat, cracking his knuckles.

"There he is," Hobart hissed, getting up and marching over to Brady.

"Come on," Zoey said, "let's collect these notes and trash them!"

Dunya and Skylar followed her, but Lily followed Hobart. She didn't know what she could do to help him— or stop him—but she knew she wanted to be there.

Brady's eyes widened when he saw Hobart, and he quickly rose and scurried away. Lily followed Hobart as he cut between tables and headed Brady off before he could leave the cafeteria.

Brady, his back against the wall, held his hands palm up. "Ryan said to do it!"

"You don't have to do everything he says! Especially when you know it's not true! That happened one time in third grade—and you did it, too."

"Whaaaat?" some kids around them said, and Brady hunched his shoulders, staring at the floor.

"And," Hobart went on, "I'm the one who got in trouble for it. I never told on you because you thought your dad wouldn't"—Hobart stopped, and saw the crowd staring at him—"never mind!"

Brady swallowed hard and blinked, staring after Hobart, who stormed back to their table.

When Lily sat down next to him, his elbows were on the table, his head in his hands, staring down.

"What did you mean about Brady's dad?" she asked gently.

Hobart sighed and spoke dully. "It was Brady's idea to pee on the playground. When the assistant principal yelled from the school and started running over, Brady said not to tell on him or his dad might never come back. He ran off, and I'm the one who got caught. Mr. Wilson asked me who the other boy was, but I didn't tell him. Brady's dad never came back, anyway."

"You're a good friend, Hobart."

"Yeah, well, Brady isn't. It was like I wasn't cool enough for him anymore. He had to have a whole stupid gang."

"It wasn't you, Hobart." Lily thought about the therapist

she saw for a while when Dad was sick and afterward, too. She told Hobart what the therapist had told her. "When a kid loses their dad—whether from death or divorce—it affects them in different ways. They're trying to figure out how to deal with it. It's not easy."

Hobart turned his head to her, still resting it in his hands. "Okay. I get it. I guess."

"It's not easy for other people, either," Lily added. "Brady hurt your feelings and that wasn't fair to you."

"None of this is fair," Zoey said, plunking down at their table, Dunya and Skylar joining her. "It's really hard to prove that you're *not* something when people have already spread rumors about you. People hear stuff and just believe it's true."

"They shouldn't," Lily said. "Anyone can say anything! That doesn't make it true at all."

"They should consider the source," Zoey said.

"What does this mean, the source?" Dunya asked.

Hobart frowned at Ryan's table. "It means, if a bully and liar like Ryan said it, it's probably not true."

"How can he get away with this?" Skylar asked.

"Because," said Zoey, "we can't prove it's Ryan and his gang."

The chimes sounded for an announcement and they heard Principal Cooper's voice. "Students! I'm very disappointed in the campaign fliers I just saw—from both sides."

"From both sides?" Hobart said, his face scrunched up. "What did *we* do?"

"All I wrote was 'Ryan is a liar' over some of the pages," Zoey said, "and that's true!"

"I'm officially wrapping up this campaign. The fifth graders have a field trip on Monday, so the speeches and elections will take place Tuesday at nine a.m. in the cafeteria."

"But it's Thursday!" Zoey said. "How can we change everyone's opinion by then?"

Hobart shook his head. "I don't think I can run. Who'll vote for me? They'll think I'm too weird."

"That we're all too weird," Skylar muttered.

"We must not let a bully win," Dunya said, her fist pounding the table.

Zoey narrowed her eyes. "She's right. We have to move forward with the campaign, no matter what."

Lily and Skylar nodded.

Hobart sighed. "Okay. On one condition. Lily, you need to be president."

"What? No! I can't!"

"You're the only one they haven't written nasty stuff about."

"Or we just haven't seen those notes yet! I'm sure they're out there."

Zoey shook her head. "Nope, I would've found them. Somehow, you got missed." She put her hands on her hips, her jaw set. "As your campaign manager, I have to agree with Hobart. Lily, you've got to be the face of the campaign."

"But I can't—"

"Also," Zoey went on, "I don't think you should speak at all, Hobart. Everyone is going to be giggling about peeing on the playground. In fact, you shouldn't even sit up there with Lily."

Hobart nodded.

Lily shook her head. "See?" she pleaded. "A speech? I can't be president because I'm too scared to give a speech, and I'm definitely not sitting in front of the whole school by myself!"

"I am sure you can do this, Lily," Dunya said, as Zoey pondered their campaign dilemma.

"Yeah," Skylar said, "if I can do it, you can do it."

"But I'll just mess up."

Zoey sighed. "Fine. Hobart, you can be up there with her, but no speech, and try not to be too noticeable."

"Okay." He turned to Lily. "Don't worry, we've all got your back. We're a team, remember?"

The others agreed and, in the end, that was the only way Lily agreed to do something that she 97 percent did *not* want to do. She stared at her shakily written name on the candidate sign-up sheet and wondered what she had done.

When she told her mother that night, Mom had insisted that Lily deserved her fifth Strive for Five charm. "If that's not stepping out of your comfort zone, I don't know what is!"

Lily shook her head. "I'm not sure why I said yes. It doesn't feel real, more like . . . impossible."

"I'm proud of you, honey, and I think it's totally possible. You can write—and deliver—a beautiful speech. You're a leader, Lily, whether you know it or not."

"I'm so *not* a leader!"

"You can be an introvert and still be a leader. Gandhi was a leader. Rosa Parks was a leader."

"I'm not like them."

"No, you're like Lily Flippin, and that's just perfect."

Lily sighed.

"You know what your dad would say, right? About speaking up? And local government?"

"I know."

Mom's voice was barely above a whisper. "He would be very proud of you, Lily."

Lily squirmed. "I haven't actually done it yet." And she wasn't sure, in the end, that she actually could.

Libro

How dare that sneeze-lurker say such things about my friends! Yes, they are my friends.

I happen to know that Skylar's father is not, nor has he ever been, in prison. Does Ryan's defense that it was simply a question absolve him of guilt? Of course not! He is planting a seed about Skylar's father. It will make people wonder, wonder about something that is totally false, but once the idea is there, minds have a way of forgetting if such information was true. Inexcusable!

Saying Hobart "pees on the playground" implies that he does so now, and regularly, not one time in third grade. Atrocious!

And warning people about Zoey, implying that she's dangerous? Reprehensible!

Finally, insinuating that being from Iraq is somehow bad because that is "all you need to know?" Abominable!

Incidentally, why is Dunya the only one without a last name? Is she not worthy? Can Ryan not be bothered to learn it or use it?

Do you see now why I call him a sneeze-lurker?

Now, before I blow my electrons all over this attic, you must excuse me while I go find that meditation program the Imaginer uses at times like this.

Only then, perhaps, will I be able to enjoy the fact that *Lily is running for president!*

Chapter 22

As Lily and Hobart approached homeroom, they saw Zoey talking to a group of kids.

"Are you kidding me? That's the reason you're voting for Ryan? Because you know him? Then you know what he's like. That's a reason to *not* vote for him!"

They had a point, though, Lily thought. No one knew her. Some kids might not like Ryan, but if they were sixth graders, they were likely to vote for him. The fifth-grade votes would be spread among the several fifth-grade candidates, so Ryan would end up with the most.

"No," Zoey was saying, throwing her head back as they walked into class, "it's a lie. A lie is still a lie no matter how many times you say it or write it in all caps on your poster. Duh."

"Well," Ava said, "not that I like him, but it's true that Hobart is only ten and Dunya is from Iraq."

"Yeah, but think about why he's saying that. He's trying to imply there's something wrong with them because of their age or where they're from. Is that fair?"

Lily knew she should be participating in the conversation if she was the one who was supposed to be president, but she was relieved that Zoey was handling things, even if she came on a little strong.

"But at least we get free ice cream if we vote for him, and a lot of other cool stuff," Samantha argued as the kids around her nodded.

Zoey stared at her. "You don't seriously believe that, do you? What is wrong with your brain? Do you even have one?"

Samantha's eyes widened as she stepped back from Zoey, turned, and headed to her desk.

Skylar tapped Zoey's arm.

She whirled around and snapped, "What?"

Skylar swallowed and said something Lily couldn't hear.

"But I'm right!" Zoey practically shouted back.

Skylar held his palm up and nodded. Either he spoke up or the class was quieting down enough for Lily to hear him. "I know, but it doesn't help if you make people feel stupid. Or yell at them." He looked down and rubbed the back of his neck. "I mean, we want them to listen to our side, right? So maybe if we're nice—"

"Okay, okay, I get it! Fine!"

Lily smiled at Skylar. She knew it was hard for him to confront people, or say anything, just like it was for her. But he was right. She was proud of him for speaking out.

"Hey, guys," Zoey said, "just wait until you hear Lily's speech! It'll be awesome!"

Lily froze. Her mind went blank. "What do I even say?" she whispered.

Hobart leaned across the aisle. "It's easy. It's all the stuff we talked about in our notes, like being respectful, thinking about world issues like climate change and immigration, and the local issues, like long lunch and lots of activities to choose from."

When Lily didn't respond, he continued, "Don't worry. You're an excellent writer. Your dad was a reporter. I bet you inherited his writing genes."

It was true. She could write. She could write well. That made her feel a bit better. Until she realized that she'd have to read her speech out loud. With everyone staring at her. Some of them, like Ryan, probably snickering.

"Okay, class," Miss Chase said, "let's get ready for math."

"Why?" Ryan said with snort. "The bell hasn't rung yet."

Miss Chase gave a long, loud exhale, stared at Ryan, and said deliberately, "It'll make up for the time you've helped us waste the first four weeks of school."

There was a murmured, "Oooh," and the entire class, except Lily, turned to look at Ryan. Lily was looking at Miss Chase, who was giving her a knowing smile. Maybe, Lily thought, Mrs. Barry had been coaching her and Miss Chase was catching on. Lily smiled back.

By the time Lily glanced back at Ryan, he'd pulled out his math book. His arms were crossed, and she couldn't tell from his expression if he was embarrassed or angry. Probably both, she decided.

In social studies, Lily and Dunya were finally in the same group, along with Iris, the girl who liked to draw. They were supposed to be discussing how a bill becomes a law, but Dunya was writing on a sheet of paper in her beautiful handwriting.

Ryan is telling lies. This is wrong. People should not tell lies.

Hobart is only ten, but does this not mean he is very smart? How many boys who are only ten do you know in grade six? Impressive!

Skylar's parents are at home and work, just like yours.

I, Dunya, am from Iraq. It is a beautiful country with a fascinating culture. Please ask me anything you want to know about it and I will tell you.

"Dunya! That's awesome!" Lily said.

Skylar was at the table next to them, his chair backing up to Dunya's. He turned around to see what they were talking about.

"Thanks, Dunya," he whispered.

"You're welcome," she said. "Ignore Ryan. Consider the source."

Lily smiled. "That's exactly right."

Dunya held up the sheet of paper when she was finished. "My tutor says she will make copies so I can post them. None of it is lies, so it's not like those other notes."

Lily was beaming, until she realized how hard others were working on the campaign. What was she doing? She should be doing something, especially if she was supposed to be president. She took a deep breath, and even though her heart was pounding, she made herself say, "Iris? Have you thought about who you're voting for in the student council election?"

"Hobart," she said, not taking her eyes off her drawing. "He'd make an awesome president." Lily thought her face went a little pink.

Dunya looked up. "It is Lily who is going to be president."

Iris stopped and adjusted her glasses. "Well, yeah, I meant Lily." Now her face was definitely pink.

"What are you girls working on?" Mrs. Barry said, and they all froze.

"Ah, I see," she said, reading over Dunya's shoulder. "The search for the truth. Admirable." She deposited protein bars on their desk and walked over to the next table, as the girls grinned.

Just before class ended, Lily saw Dunya sweep up the protein bars at their table and silently deposit them in Skylar's open backpack behind her.

At lunch, Zoey showed them a new Get REAL poster.

Get
Ready.
Elect
A
Lily!

Lily groan-sighed. "Does it have to say my name?"

"Duh," Zoey said, "you're the president! They have to know your name. Now I need to put them up."

Dunya followed Zoey to post what she'd written in social studies.

Hobart invited Lily to "work the crowd" with him but she made an excuse about staying at the table in case someone came to see her.

The Hammer sat down next to Skylar and put his lunch box on the table. "Folks, I have some news. My grandson is having health issues, so my wife and I are moving down to Florida to be near my daughter and her family."

"You're leaving?" Skylar's voice cracked. "For good?"

Mr. Hammer pressed his lips together and nodded.

Lily couldn't help looking around the cafeteria for Hobart. He was going to be crushed by this news.

"I'll be back to visit, but my job here is over. And you know what? I think you kids are going to be just fine. You've got your own team now."

Skylar gave a nod. "I guess."

"Skylar, I hope you'll do me the honor of taking my Black Panther lunch box since I won't be needing it anymore."

Skylar's face lit up. "Thanks."

"And Lily," the Hammer said, "I'm proud of you. I told my wife about you strong girls and, since she has every arts and crafts item you can imagine, she made these buttons for you."

Mr. Hammer handed her a bunch of buttons that said Flip for Flippin!

"Wow," Lily breathed, "these are great. Thank you."

"You're welcome. She expects you to win, though," he added with a wink.

"I'll try."

"Now, if you'll excuse me, I have to go see my man, Hobart."

"Wait!" Lily said, suddenly remembering something. "I was supposed to learn curling so I could tell you all about it. I never did!"

"Don't worry," Mr. Hammer said with a chuckle. "Hobart gave me the name of that curling book he read. The important part is that Hobart has a friend, a whole group of friends." He smiled. "Sometimes it feels like you don't quite fit right in school, but school isn't real life. Hobart is going to ace real life." He looked from Lily to Skylar and back to Lily. "You all are."

Lily felt herself smiling and saw that Skylar was, too. She watched the Hammer walk over to Hobart and saw them high-five. After that, though, the grin dropped from Hobart's face, his shoulders drooped, and he seemed to shrink smaller and smaller the more Mr. Hammer spoke. They walked to the end of an almost empty table and sat down as the Hammer kept talking. Finally, Hobart returned, head down, to their table.

"Look, aren't these cool?" Lily said, showing him the Flip for Flippin buttons. She didn't even know why she was saying it, except that she wanted to try to cheer up her friend. "And he gave Skylar his Black Panther lunch box. Isn't that great?" She couldn't seem to stop herself. "What did he give you?"

Hobart glanced behind him to watch the Hammer talking to Dunya and Zoey. "Superpowers."

Skylar nodded like that made complete sense.

"I'm going to miss him," Hobart said.

Skylar nodded again.

Lily sighed. "We all are."

They watched him as he was leaving the cafeteria, but he turned toward them at the door, crossed his arms in an X over his chest, and called out, "Wakanda forever!"

Hobart and Skylar both stood up, crossing their arms against their chests. "Wakanda forever!"

Dunya and Zoey returned to their table, Dunya saying, "I'm so sorry Mr. Hammer is leaving."

"I know," Zoey said. "I wish Ryan were the one leaving. Now that he can't hand out notes with lies, he has his gang out telling lies for him."

Hobart whipped his head around to Ryan's table. "Perfect! He's alone!" He quickly stalked over to Ryan.

"What's he doing?" Dunya asked, a tremor in her voice.

"I don't know," Lily said, instinctively looking around for Mr. Hammer because this did not look good, but realizing he was gone. They were on their own now.

Ryan sneered, but Lily noticed he quickly looked toward the cafeteria door before facing Hobart. "What do you want, Ho-fart?"

Hobart put his hands on the table and leaned over to Ryan.

Ryan actually pulled back in his seat a little, even though he was still sneering.

Lily, and all of them, watched.

"Go, Hobart!" Zoey said, under her breath.

They couldn't hear anything Hobart said. He looked

like a teacher, leaning over Ryan, who never said anything, just wore his sneer. That was exactly what it looked like to Lily, too, that Ryan was wearing a plastered-on sneer rather than a real one.

Lily heard Dunya let out her breath when Hobart turned and began walking back to them. Lily let out her breath, too, and looking down at her sandwich, realized that she'd held it so tight, her fingers had squished through the bread.

"I thought you were going to fight him," Dunya told Hobart, with a sigh of relief.

He shook his head. "I wanted to talk to him without anyone around because I didn't want to embarrass him."

"Seriously?" Zoey said.

"Yeah. Think about it. If he's embarrassed, he'll just make fun of me. If I can talk to him alone, he might actually listen."

"How did you stay so calm?" Lily asked.

"I was the Hammer. Do you notice how he's always quiet and calm, but his words are like hammers going bam, bam, bam?"

Lily had.

"That's how I did it."

Skylar nodded. "Superpowers."

Hobart finally smiled. "Yup."

"Hey, moron!" Ryan yelled.

Lily groaned inwardly but then saw that Ryan wasn't

looking at Hobart. He was glaring at Brady, who held a tray of food.

"You're supposed to be campaigning for me," Ryan told him. "Go!"

Brady hesitated, turning away from Ryan's table and ending up looking at Lily's.

She caught his eye and, instead of instinctively looking away, Lily held his gaze for several moments. She looked around her table quickly and everyone was chatting. "Hobart?"

"What?" He was giving Skylar a thumbs-up on the Black Panther lunch box.

"I have an idea. Why don't you ask Brady to join us?"

"Are you kidding? I'm not asking him! I can't believe we used to be friends."

Zoey stared at Lily. "You do realize he's a total brat, right?"

Skylar had turned to look at Brady, who was still frozen in the middle of the cafeteria.

"I don't think he wants to be a brat, though," Lily said. "I'm—I'm going to go ask him." She stood up, though it felt like a weight was on her.

"I will go also," Dunya said.

It felt good to have someone with her. "Brady?" Lily's voice squeaked and she cleared her throat. "You can sit at our table."

Brady leaned away from her. He eyed Hobart, Zoey, and Skylar as if he thought they'd yell "Go!" at him, like Ryan had.

Lily turned to look at them, too. Hobart was ignoring them. Zoey was eating. Skylar tilted his head at Brady, moved his lunch bag over, and patted the table twice.

"See?" Lily said. "It's okay."

Brady chewed his lip.

Lily and Dunya looked at each other. Lily could feel Ryan's eyes on her.

"Come, Brady," Dunya said in a calm voice, "you are welcome with us."

He shook his head. "Hobart won't say that."

After what seemed like forever, Dunya sighed and gave Lily a shrug before turning and going back to the table.

Lily didn't want to give up. At the same time, she was angry with Brady for the way he treated Hobart. "Look!" she said, the strength of her voice surprising her, as well as Brady, who jerked his head up, eyeing her warily.

"You've been mean to Hobart for a really long time. You can't expect him to like you instantly. You have to earn his friendship. I can tell you this, though: his friendship is totally worth it." She folded her arms and gave Brady a mom stare.

He blinked at her and, finally, gave enough of a head movement that Lily took it as a nod and led the way to her table. She worried whether Hobart would welcome them. He was watching them approach, but he wasn't smiling.

Lily pleaded with him with her eyes.

Hobart looked at the ceiling and gave a long exhale. He pulled a plastic container from his lunch box, and slowly laid a large, homemade chocolate chunk cookie at everyone's place—including the spot Skylar had made for Brady.

Libro

*H*obart is IN the HOUSE! Did you see him go over and confront Ryan? That was, as you humans say, awesome! Words are strong. Also . . . a superpower. Well done, Hobart!

And kudos to Lily, too. Asking Brady to join their table was not a popular move with Ryan or even some of her own friends. It's hard trying to do the right thing when even your supporters aren't, well, supporting you. I daresay they will see that Lily is right. I suspect Brady will become a grateful, and loyal, member of their team.

I am sad, indeed, to see the Hammer go. He may be right that everyone will be fine, but I shall still miss him. Fortunately, he left some of his superpowers with Hobart.

On a lighter note, I must say I like *Flip for Flippin.* Do

you think the Imaginer made Lily's last name Flippin so she could use that slogan? That would be a good guess. However, that is not the case. The Imaginer borrowed it from her fourth-grade friend Virginia Flippin, whose campaign she supported. And yes, they even had posters and buttons that said *Flip for Flippin.* Sadly, young Ms. Flippin did not win. In that story. Who knows what will happen in this one?

Chapter 23

As they walked home Friday afternoon, Lily counted her Strive for Five achievements. She'd yelled "Manitoba tuck" to save Hobart, asked Mrs. Barry to help Miss Chase, invited kids to her lunch table so they weren't sitting alone, stood up for Hobart against Ryan by saying "Ho-BART" and "Girls make excellent friends," and now, somehow, she was a candidate for president of the student council.

Still, she wasn't sure she was doing the right thing. In fact, she was feeling a little sick. She stopped walking and Hobart bumped into her.

"Sorry!" he said. "What's up?"

"I'm having second thoughts about running for president."

"You're going to be great!" Hobart said, as he'd said numerous times before.

It occurred to Lily that, although Hobart knew she was shy, he didn't really understand what it was like because *he* wasn't shy. Maybe it had been hard for him to stand up to his dad and to Ryan, but he had done it. He was much braver than Lily.

Dunya seemed to understand her anxiety better. "You are a quiet person," she said. "Of course it is frightening to stand up in front of everyone and speak. You must pretend that you are speaking to one person only. On Tuesday, I will sit at our table in the middle of the cafeteria so you can look at me. But first, I will help you practice. You will say your speech to me many times so you will feel more comfortable when Tuesday comes."

In fact, Lily had arranged for Dunya to spend the night on Saturday. Not only would they go over her speech, Mom was also taking them to the mall for Lily to choose a new dress for the occasion. She smiled. She had completed Dad's Strive for Five *and* was honoring Dad's other wish for her, to find a girl to be a friend because *girls make excellent friends.*

Dunya brought up the details of the sleepover before they reached Farouk's school. "I'll be ready tomorrow after one o'clock, but my mother says I must be home early on Sunday morning."

"Wait," Hobart said, "we're having a sleepover?"

Both girls giggled.

"Not we," Lily said, "just Dunya and I."

"Oh, right," Hobart said, dropping his head.

"I mean," Lily tried to explain, "it would be weird to have a boy at a sleepover."

"Yes, girls only," Dunya said.

"Dunya's going to listen to me say my speech over and over," Lily said, "and we're going shopping because my mom's buying me a new dress for Tuesday."

Hobart still didn't look at her. "That's cool."

Lily and Dunya shared a look. "Do you want to come to the speech part?" Lily said.

"Nah, my dad's going shopping for the new truck, so I'll help him with that. We're looking at brochures tonight. We might even start looking at them now. Is it okay if I don't walk Skippy with you?"

Lily was surprised, but said it was fine. She watched him walk away as she and Dunya turned toward the elementary school.

"I hope I didn't hurt his feelings."

Dunya shook her head. "But a boy-girl sleepover would definitely not work. Not with my mother!"

Lily thought about how difficult it had been for Mom to convince Dunya's mother to let her stay overnight. Mom had finally won over Mrs. Hassan by saying, "We're all girls here."

The next day, Lily and her mother picked Dunya up and

went straight to the mall. Not only did they find a dress, they had lunch in the food court and smoothies afterward. They wandered in and out of stores, tried not to laugh at overly dramatic teens, and giggled a lot. Lily noticed her mom watching them and smiling. Lily's friendship with Dunya was even making Mom happy.

They spent the rest of the afternoon with Lily practicing her speech. Over and over. Lily was determined to memorize it. Sometimes Mom watched, sometimes not. Her mother couldn't resist saying things like "Speak up, honey" and "Try to make eye contact with someone in the audience."

"That's what I *am* doing, Mom," Lily finally said, adding pointedly, "with Dunya."

Mom nodded. "Got it. I'm going to go start on salad and order a pizza, since that's what the presidential candidate and the secretary have declared."

Dunya giggled. "Thank you, Mrs. Flippin."

"You're very welcome." Mom turned before entering the kitchen. "And Lily? You're doing great. Dad would be so proud. I am, too."

They finally took a break and threw balls for Skippy. Dunya threw one over the fence.

Lily was impressed. "You should try out for softball!"

Dunya laughed as she went to retrieve the ball and got stuck at the gate. "As long as I do not need to get out of a gate!"

Lily opened it for her, saying, "Don't latch it. It's too hard to open."

Skippy barked and they saw the pizza delivery girl drive up.

"Come on, Skippy!" Lily called. "Let's go inside."

Skippy was the first to the kitchen door.

When they sat down at the kitchen table, Mom looked at the empty fourth chair. "Where's Hobart?"

Both girls giggled.

"What?" Mom looked at them blankly.

"Mom, he can't come to a sleepover!"

"No, but he could've come for dinner. Pizza is his favorite."

"Oh." Suddenly, Lily felt guilty. Pizza *was* Hobart's favorite.

"He is looking at new trucks," Dunya told Lily's mom, explaining how grateful her family was that Mr. Hall was going to give them his current truck.

Mom seemed to sense that Lily felt bad and, after making popcorn, she kept them playing board games and cards all evening, even teaching Dunya their family's version of rummy.

"You made up this game yourselves?"

"It's just a slight variation," Mom said, "and sometimes we make up silly rules as we go along."

Lily nodded, adding, "Like, you can say 'freeze' if you don't want a player to pick up your discard so you can stop them from going out first and winning."

Mom smirked and raised her eyebrows. "That didn't work on your father, though, did it?"

Lily grinned at Mom, then at Dunya. "My dad would always sigh or get confused—"

"It was all an act," Mom broke in.

"Right, because he always put down his whole hand first, saying, 'Is this it? I'm not sure. . . .'"

Dunya clapped both hands down on the table. "Yes! This is what my grandmother does! She pretends she doesn't understand a game when she plays with my brother and I, but then she wins and says, 'Oh, I didn't know. I must be lucky.'"

"Your grandmother and my dad would've gotten along great."

Dunya gave a conspiratorial smile. "Just recently, she told me she does it to teach Farouk how to lose with grace." She sat back and rolled her eyes. "He still needs a lot of practice."

Mom laughed. "Well, maybe he can come over with you sometime and we'll all play. At least he'll have a fair chance to win or lose. And it's fun to play with even more people."

Lily thought about Hobart. Why had they never taught him how to play Zany Rummy? She made a note to herself that she needed to do that the very next time he was over.

When all three of them were yawning, Mom announced

it was bedtime. "I know it's only nine thirty, but you girls will be up chatting for a while, I'm sure."

Skippy scratched at the kitchen door to go out, staring at Mom, who was yawning again.

"I'll take care of him," Lily said.

Mom was right about them chatting. They sprawled on Lily's bed as she asked Dunya all about her home, school, and life in Iraq.

When Dunya sighed, Lily stopped herself. "I'm sorry! I'm asking you too many questions."

"No, no, it's fine. I just felt sad for a moment, thinking about my friends."

"We can talk about something else."

"Actually," Dunya said, smoothing the comforter, "it's nice to talk about them. Most people don't want to know, or at least, they don't ask. Even if they do, they're not as interested as you are."

"I can't imagine not wanting to know. I love trying to understand other cultures!"

"Me, too."

"You know so much already, Dunya. You'd be excellent in a geography bee."

"How do we do this bee?"

Lily explained how it worked and how much fun it was just to learn, adding, "If you want, you can compete to represent your school, and state, and even go to the national bee, in Washington, except we don't have to do that part."

"Why not? We are strong, smart girls. This is what my mother says. We did not leave our country and come to America to be average. We come here to excel."

Lily fiddled with her bracelet and said nothing.

"Why do you look unhappy?"

"My dad . . . we . . . he wanted me to participate in the bee, but I didn't want to. He was sick and I wanted to spend all my time with him."

"But you know a lot about geography. I thought you did this bee already."

Lily shook her head. Looking at her new friend, she slowly got up and pulled her geography box out of her closet. She wasn't exactly sure why, except that she wanted to share something special with Dunya. That was what friends did.

Lily was rewarded by Dunya's enthusiasm as she sifted through the box. "It's a pop-up Taj Mahal! You made this?"

Lily nodded.

"Oh, this is a beautiful map! You made it, too?"

"Yes. It has different colors to show ethnic groups, which aren't the same as country borders."

"Very true," Dunya said. She picked up Lily's geography journal. "May I look?"

"Sure," Lily said, looking over Dunya's shoulder, as she flipped through the pages.

"You have learned a lot! Your father wrote these—'Lily

learned all the capitals in Asia!' He was very proud." She turned to the next page. "There is no date here." Dunya turned the journal and held it up for Lily to see. *Lily participated in GeoBee!*

"I know. Because I never did it."

"Yet," Dunya said, gently closing the book. "Now you will."

Lily shrugged. "Maybe."

"You must. It's important to do this," Dunya said gently, "to honor your father."

Lily nodded slowly. "Okay, but Mrs. Barry says she needs help and wants me to be her assistant. I don't mind making up questions, but I don't like organizing people into groups and giving them assignments. I bet you could do that. Would you mind being co-assistants?"

"Of course! We will talk to Mrs. Barry on Monday."

Lily was still fingering her bracelet, and Dunya said, "That is very beautiful. Tell me about it."

"My dad gave it to me with the Labradoodle charm, and I earned all the others."

"How?"

"Dad challenged me to Strive for Five, which meant speaking up five times because he said each time I did, it would get easier."

"That is very wise. So how did you earn each one of these?"

"Well, the state charm is for yelling a warning to

Hobart in the middle of the cafeteria, the United States is for asking Mrs. Barry to help Miss Chase handle our class, North America is for . . . well . . . asking you and Skylar to join our table."

Dunya grinned.

"The globe is for talking back to Ryan—with your help. And the universe is for running for president."

Dunya fingered the charm of North America. "This is my favorite one."

Lily smiled. "It's my favorite, too."

The next morning, when Mom woke them up, Lily didn't even remember falling asleep.

"Is Skippy in here with you?" Mom asked.

"No," Lily said, with a yawn.

"Are you sure? He's not inside. And I don't see him outside, either."

"What?" Lily tried to remember. She'd let him out last night and . . . assumed that Mom let him in because he hadn't scratched at the door or barked. "Did you let him in last night?"

"No," Mom said, "I thought you said you were taking care of him."

Lily's stomach tightened.

She jumped out of bed and ran to the yard, yelling "Skippy!" *Oh, please be here, please be here, please be here.*

Then she saw the open gate.

Dunya, who had followed her outside, gasped. "That was my fault!"

"No, it wasn't," Lily said. "I told you to leave it like that."

Mom was on the stoop. "The gate wasn't latched?"

Lily felt the tears come hard and fast. "I'm sorry, Mom." She was gulp crying now. "It's all my fault!"

"Lily, honey, it's okay. I'm sure he's fine."

But Lily could tell from Mom's worried expression that she wasn't sure at all.

"I'm going to run Dunya home, and I'll look for him while I'm out."

"I'm coming with you," Lily said, wiping her eyes.

"No, you stay here in case he comes back. Then bring him inside and lock the door and—and give him some left-over pizza."

Now Lily knew Mom was worried.

Dunya gave her a hug and said some kind of prayer or hopeful words in Arabic.

"Call Hobart!" Mom said as she ran out the door. "Skippy loves that boy. Maybe he found Hobart's house!"

Lily dialed Hobart's number, and Mrs. Hall answered. Lily explained what had happened. There was a fumbling sound and Hobart was on the phone. "How long has he been gone?"

"I don't even know, Hobart." Lily started to cry again.

"Hang on. I'll be right over."

She dressed and was outside before Hobart had reached the gate. "I'm supposed to stay in case Skippy comes back, but I can't just sit here! I have to go look. It's all my fault!"

"Okay," Hobart said, "I have my mom's phone in case we need to call anyone. She's out driving the streets and we're supposed to look anywhere a car can't go."

They ran down the street, looking behind people's bushes and under the cars, calling for Skippy. Lily realized the direction they were headed. She and Hobart looked at each other at the same moment and both said, "The park!"

A few minutes later, they found Skippy lying next to an overflowing trash can.

He wasn't moving.

Libro

W hat?!

    Crikey! They are strange humans these Imaginers. Why do they always want to kill off the dogs? I think it's unconscionable, don't you? I know the Imaginer has had beloved dogs who've left this world, so she has experienced that painful loss, but I ask you, does that give her the right to put the rest of us through such agony?

I think not! In fact, I demand that she not do this.

Therefore, I want you to think—no, shout—Don't kill Skippy!

Can you do that?

Try it.

DON'T KILL SKIPPY!

Oh, come on, she'll never hear you. You can do better than that.

Try it again.

Better.

One more time, with gusto.

Well done. Let us hope that works.

Chapter 24

"Skippy!" Lily screamed, falling on her knees next to him.

Skippy's eyes fluttered open then closed again.

"You're okay, Skippy," Hobart said, scooped him up in his arms, and somehow carried him to the park gate, just as Hobart's dad drove up in a brand-new truck.

"Your mom said—"

"Dad! We need to get him to the vet now!"

Mr. Hall picked up Skippy as Lily and Hobart climbed in the back seat. He lay the dog across their laps, then called Lily's mom to tell her they were on the way to the emergency vet. Lily was crying too much to speak.

"It's okay," Hobart was saying, to Lily or Skippy; Lily wasn't sure. "Everything's going to be fine."

"Skippy," Lily whispered through her tears, "please hang on!"

Lily tried to talk to Skippy when she wasn't crying. The only thing that kept her going was Hobart's soothing voice, talking to Skippy nonstop, and the fact that he was there.

At the vet, Hobart insisted on holding on to Skippy, only letting his dad help because the dog was so heavy. Lily blurted out that Skippy must've eaten some trash at the park.

"We've got him!" a male tech called out, and he followed a female tech down the hall, carrying Skippy. "Wait in there." He nodded at an open door.

A receptionist held out a clipboard with forms on it. "Can someone fill this in?"

Hobart called over his shoulder, "You do it, Dad! I have to go with Lily."

"Uh . . . I don't . . . I . . . Okay," Mr. Hall said.

Lily and Hobart sat in the exam room together, their shoulders touching.

"What do you think they're doing?" Lily said through tears.

"Saving him," Hobart said confidently.

"Are you sure?"

"Positive," Hobart said.

A tech, the name Annie embroidered on her blue scrubs,

knocked on the door, entered, and knelt down in front of them. "We did an X-ray and there's something lodged in his stomach. The doctor is deciding whether he needs surgery or an endoscopy—that's removing what's in his stomach without having to make an incision."

"Will he be okay?" Lily began crying again.

Annie handed her a box of tissues and smiled. "I think he'll be fine. He's young and healthy. I'll be back shortly to let you know how it went."

Lily wiped her eyes and gripped her charm bracelet. "Thanks for helping, Hobart."

"Of course."

"And I'm sorry about having Dunya over. I didn't mean to ignore you. I wish I'd told you to come for pizza last—"

"It's okay," Hobart said. "I get that girls want to hang out together sometimes. Same with boys. I wasn't upset about that."

"What were you upset about?"

"I don't know. . . . That you said I was weird."

"I didn't say that!"

"Yeah, you said I was weird about the whole sleepover thing."

"No, I meant it would be weird to have a boy at a girl's sleepover, that's all."

Hobart shrugged, looking at the floor. "And I guess I was a little jealous that you were so happy to hang out with

Dunya and you didn't think about me at all."

That stung Lily, all the more so because he was right. She tried to explain how Dad had wanted her to find a friend, but it sounded rather silly when she said that girls make excellent friends.

"Did he say that boys *don't* make excellent friends?"

"No. I think . . . I don't know. As shy as I was with girls, I was even shyer with boys. Maybe he thought it'd be easier for me to make friends with a girl, sort of like me, who was quiet and . . . Well, anyway, I've figured out one thing. A friend is someone who's there for you. That's you, Hobart."

"That's you, too, Lily."

Lily's shoulders sagged. She hadn't been there for him. "You're making me feel worse."

Hobart grinned. "Good, then it's working."

Lily couldn't help smiling back. She finally let go of her charm bracelet.

"Hey," Hobart said, looking at her bracelet, "what's that new one with colors?"

"It's the universe. That's for running for president."

Hobart nodded. "You know what? You having Dunya over made me think about asking Skylar . . . and Brady . . . over sometime. Who knows? Maybe I can start a curling team."

"Don't you need four people?"

"Yeah, but you can play with three if you have to—hey! You were paying attention about curling!"

"I have an awesome teacher."

Hobart gave her a smile. "You can also play mixed doubles. With you, Dunya, and Zoey, we have three girls and three boys so that's three teams. For mixed doubles there are only eight ends—that's like an inning—instead of ten, and you only use six stones instead of eight, although, really, it's just five because you have to put one of your stones on the center line. Did you get all that?"

"Aye-aye, captain," Lily said.

"Actually, the captain is called the skip."

"Skip? Like Skippy?"

"Where are they?" It was Mom's voice in the lobby.

Lily jumped up and opened the door. "We're in here, Mom! It's okay. Skippy's going to be all right."

It looked like Mom was going to melt into a puddle on the floor, but she was smiling.

A while later, the vet allowed them to see Skippy, who was still groggy from anesthesia. He thumped his tail weakly.

"Skippy! You're—" Lily was too choked up to say anything else.

Hobart finished for her, "*In* the *house!*"

Libro

Excellent work, smart reader! She did not kill the dog. You saved Skippy!

Now, if you were one of those people who wanted the dog to die, you can just move on to a different book. This one's not for you. And incidentally, if you did want the dog to die—what is wrong with you?? A dog is a person's most faithful friend. Well, in addition to humans.

Chapter 25

That night, Hobart came over for dinner and Mom ordered pizza. He told them how, after he and his dad got home from the vet, they'd taken their old truck to the church.

"Dunya was there with her dad. She was excited about Skippy but nervous because of, well, my dad. He just gave her a nod, though, and actually shook hands with her dad. And they talked for, like, two minutes, while I showed Dunya the broken cupholder, so no one has a drink spill all over themselves like I did. Anyway, when we were walking home, he said Dunya's dad was a good man, and that's a lot, coming from my dad!"

"I am so pleased to hear that," Mom said.

Lily raised her eyebrows at Hobart. "Who knows, maybe your dad will end up liking him."

Hobart smirked. "I forgot to ask if he likes hockey."

After dinner, they taught Hobart how to play Zany Rummy, which Hobart said they had to teach kids at school because it was such fun. Eventually, since Mom had work to do, Lily and Hobart went in the living room. Lily ran through her speech so Hobart could hear it.

Afterward, she couldn't seem to sit, or even stand, still.

Hobart sat on the couch with Skippy's head in his lap. "Why are you pacing?"

"I'm worried about my speech."

"You don't need to worry," Hobart said. "You've already memorized it. And it's good! And, anyway, it's not until Tuesday."

"But I'm really nervous already." She paused after turning around at the living room wall again. "I've done my Strive for Five challenge, and it was supposed to get easier to step out of my comfort zone." She shook her head and resumed pacing. "But it's not. I'm dreading giving my speech. How can I be so scared when I've already spoken up five times? Strive for Five didn't work."

Hobart grinned slowly.

"What?"

"Don't you see? It already has."

She stood still, staring at him. "What do you mean?"

Hobart sat up. "A month ago, would you even have considered running for student council president?"

"No way!"

Hobart gently slid Skippy off his lap onto the couch and jumped up. "And here you are!"

Lily considered that. She saw his point, but . . . "It's really scary, though. It's supposed to get easier."

Hobart gave a shrug. "I think the little things are probably easier. This is a big thing, and it's okay to be scared. But remember, you have a whole team behind you. You can do it."

After Hobart left that evening, Lily thought how much Hobart was like Dad. When someone knows you like that, you know you've found a true friend.

Monday morning flew by. Lily couldn't decide whether that was a good thing, because she didn't have to spend so much time being nervous, or a bad thing, because it meant Tuesday morning, and giving her speech, was even closer. The only time she'd spoken much was when she and Dunya talked to a delighted Mrs. Barry about the geography bee club.

"Two helpers!" Mrs. Barry said. "It doesn't get any better than that!"

On their way to lunch, Dunya clutched her arm. "This is going to be fun!"

Lily agreed, although she knew she'd feel more excited after the elections.

Brady joined them at their lunch table. He didn't say anything, even when they all said hi, but Lily figured it was a start. Zoey had told her it was a brilliant tactical maneuver, recruiting someone from the enemy side, but that's not why Lily had done it. She felt sorry for Brady. He was a little like her, maybe. He didn't seem to really know how to make friends or join another group. He couldn't seem to speak up for himself. She knew what that was like, and she wanted to help him. She also hoped that, since he and Hobart had been such good friends, maybe they could be friends again.

"Would everyone like to see the newsletter my tutor, Miss Hinojosa, and I put together?" Dunya asked.

"Of course!" Zoey said as the others agreed.

Dunya took several copies out of her backpack. Lily noticed she slid one directly in front of Brady and gave him a smile.

Lily looked at the bright, clear font and columns. "This is awesome!"

There was an announcements section as well as entertainment, where all the lunchtime activities would be listed, a sports section, and a calendar. "Because," Dunya explained, "Miss Hinojosa said not everyone can see the school website and also if people see things several times they will remember." She added, "Is it okay if I add an idea?"

"Sure!" Hobart said.

"I would like to have an international dinner at school

one night, where everyone brings foods from their country. My grandmother says that food brings people together."

"I love that," Lily said. "And it goes with our whole idea of getting to know people and understanding your community."

"Yeah," Hobart said. "Nobody's an outsider."

"Nobody's a weirdo," Skylar added.

Lily nodded. "Once we get to know each other better."

Zoey gave a heavy sigh. "Okay, guys, I hate to say this, but not everyone is going to like everyone else. For two weeks at summer camp they can make you do that, or pretend to do that, but you do know that school isn't going to suddenly be all campfires and 'Kumbaya,' right?"

"I know," Lily said. "All I want is for people to not be mean to each other and at least accept each other. We don't all have to be best friends."

"Good," said Zoey, "because I, for one, don't want to be friends with Ryan!"

Lily noticed Brady look at his hands and start picking at his nails. She cleared her throat. "I'd like to know the *why* behind his meanness."

"Yeah," Hobart agreed.

After a moment, Brady muttered, barely audibly, "His dad."

Hobart turned to him. "What do you mean?"

Brady shrugged, but he glanced at Skylar and quickly looked down again.

What does Skylar have to do with Ryan's dad? Lily wondered.

Dunya folded her arms and sat back. "Now I understand."

"What?" said Zoey.

Dunya looked at Brady. "It is Ryan's father who is a thief and may go to jail, isn't it." She didn't say it as a question, though.

Brady kept his head down but gave a nod.

"Whoa," Hobart said slowly, "how did you figure that out, Dunya?"

"When people accuse you of bad things, it is often because *they* would do those bad things, or maybe already have."

Lily thought about what Ryan's mom had said that day she'd visited their classroom. It was something about *you'll* have a chance to turn out right. Lily realized that Mrs. King wasn't talking about Ryan versus other kids. She was talking about Ryan versus his dad.

"Well," Zoey said, "the apple doesn't fall far from the tree."

Brady snapped his head up as he clutched his stomach.

Lily saw Dunya's eyebrows knit together, so she explained, "It means Ryan is like his father."

Dunya shook her head slowly. "He is just a boy. He is confused. He can change."

Zoey raised her eyebrows and pressed her lips together.

"It doesn't seem possible," Hobart said, "but my dad is changing—some—and he's old."

"Okay," Zoey said, "but I don't like who Ryan is right now."

"It's hard to like someone who acts that way," Skylar said softly. "We just have to not hate him or it doesn't give him a chance to change."

They all decided they could agree on that.

That night, Mom put Lily's favorite lemon cake batter in the oven and started making the lemon frosting.

"What's this for?"

Mom took out the hand mixer and plugged it in. "We're celebrating your victory."

"Mom, the election is tomorrow. And we're not going to win, anyway, probably."

Mom raised her eyebrows. "We don't *know* who's going to win. And, anyway, what we're celebrating is your completion of Strive for Five, and beyond." Mom set the mixer down on the counter. "I mean, look at you, Lily. Look how far you've come. I couldn't be prouder." Mom's eyes welled up and she pressed her lips together, gazing at Lily, then pulled her into a hug.

Lily knew Mom wanted to add how proud Dad would be, too, but she had to stop herself from crying. It was okay. Lily knew.

After dinner, Lily could only manage a small piece of cake. She promised Mom she'd feel like eating two or three pieces after school on Tuesday.

Mom scraped some frosting off her plate and licked her fork before putting it down. "Maybe Hobart would like some? And Dunya and Farouk? I'll come home early tomorrow. You all deserve to celebrate, whatever the outcome. And how about this: Why don't you see if all your friends can come over sometime this weekend?"

All your friends. Lily smiled. "Okay. Thanks, Mom."

Later, Lily read the letter from her dad. "I'm trying," she whispered. "I wish you were here to see it."

She wore her charm bracelet, with all five charms, to bed, which she normally didn't do, but clutching on to it helped her fall asleep.

Libro

Please, let Lily be president. Can you imagine that sneeze-lurker as president? Deliver us from that! Even the Imaginer cannot have that warped of an imagination to let a bully become president.

Chapter 26

On their way to school the next morning, Hobart spent half the time walking backward. It was partly because Lily was walking slowly, and he kept getting ahead of her. It was also because of his energy level.

"Sorry, this is how I get when I'm excited!"

"Hobart, we don't know if we're going to win. We probably won't."

"Yeah, but we're going for it. No one stopped us. Not even Ryan. That's like a win already." He jumped and spun in the air as if trying a basketball layup. "Plus, we're going to do the activity tables in the cafeteria no matter what." He stopped abruptly. "Hey! I can take a table and teach people about curling!" He smacked his forehead. "Why didn't I think of that before?" He did an impromptu Manitoba tuck, then continued walking, practically dancing. "This is awesome!"

They went straight to the cafeteria, since those students giving speeches were allowed to arrive first and prepare. They met Dunya and Skylar at their usual table.

Dunya gave Lily a hug. "I'm going to be right here, so tell me your speech like you did on Saturday."

Skylar was clutching his arms around his chest and looked even paler than usual.

Hobart glanced at Lily. "Hey, Skylar, you want to help me wheel some chairs in from the library? There are seven teams, so we need fourteen chairs for each president and vice president. Come on."

Skylar, arms still wrapped around himself, haltingly followed Hobart out of the cafeteria.

Lily turned to Dunya. "You look so calm."

Dunya smiled. "I am nervous. But it is not the scariest thing I have ever done."

Of course, Lily realized, fleeing your home and being a refugee couldn't even compare to this. Still, it didn't help her feel less nervous.

In fact, as kids started filing into the cafeteria, Lily felt like she was the eye of a hurricane, a roaring flurry of activity spinning around her, except that instead of being the calm center, she was quivering. Someone brave, like Zoey, should be doing this.

Lily glanced around the room for Zoey. Eventually, she saw their campaign manager pointing to a Get REAL poster and explaining it to a group of kids.

"Fifth grade! Miss Robinson's class!" a teacher barked. "Move all the way down! Fill in those gaps! No saving seats for friends. This isn't a chatting opportunity. You're here to listen to the candidates!"

Lily swallowed. *The candidates.* And she was one of them.

"I'm voting for you," Brady said. It felt like he appeared out of nowhere. But there was Hobart, next to him, a hand on Brady's shoulder, saying, "He's on our team now."

Brady smiled and Lily realized how pained his face had always looked. Until now.

Skylar was also there, on the other side of Hobart. "Good luck," he whispered.

Lily forced a smile. "Good luck to you, too."

Skylar's face went paler than usual. "I—I'm not sure I can give the speech."

Lily and Hobart looked at each other for an answer.

"Yeah, you can," Brady said softly. "Remember what Mr. Hammer always used to say? Wakanda forever, right?"

Skylar didn't say anything but nodded slowly.

Lily smiled at Brady, who gave a shrug.

"Take your seats, everyone," Mrs. Cooper called out.

Lily looked at Hobart, who was dressed up for the occasion. Her face must've shown her fear because he said, "It's okay, you can do this. Really."

He gently nudged her into one of the chairs at the front of the cafeteria and sat down next to her. They both noticed Skylar still standing in the same spot, frozen.

"I'll be right back," Hobart said, jumping up and steering Skylar back toward their lunch table.

Ryan sat on the other side of Lily. "Loser," he whispered. "You should've listened to me the first day."

Lily felt herself sink into the chair. What was she thinking? Trying to be student council president? If she'd listened to Ryan, she wouldn't be sitting here. How could she possibly—then she saw Hobart, grinning and high-fiving Skylar and Brady, Zoey doing a little victory dance, and Dunya laughing. If she had listened to Ryan, she wouldn't have her friends, her team. She turned in her seat and gave him a mom stare.

"Oh, yeah, I'm really worried now," Ryan mocked, rolling his eyes and smirking.

You should be, Lily thought.

Hobart ran up and sat on the other side of Lily.

Ryan smirked at him. "Hi, Ho—"

"Bart!" Hobart said, loudly, like a cheer.

Ryan frowned.

Lily looked at the row of fifth graders facing her. They were only six feet away. A girl with pigtails, wearing a plaid skirt and tights, was waving at her. Lily recognized her as the girl who had refused to take free ice cream from Ryan because she was offended by his bribery. She waved back.

"Who is she?" the girl's friend said, eyeing Lily.

The girl in pigtails grinned. "She could be our next president!"

Lily felt slightly woozy. She craned her neck to search for Dunya and couldn't find her. Or Skylar. Or Zoey. Or Brady. "Where are they?" she breathed.

"There," Hobart said, pointing.

"Where?"

He leaned in front of Lily to catch her eye, then pointed again. "Right there."

It still took her a moment, but finally she saw Zoey. She was standing and waving.

"Good," she murmured, giving a nod.

Mrs. Cooper introduced the speakers and the first fifth-grade candidate began. He was so nervous, he dropped his speech twice, lost his place, and sat down without finishing. Lily felt bad for him, but it also gave her some encouragement. She wasn't the only one who was shaking.

The rest of the fifth-grade candidates stood up with their vice presidents, some of whom gave speeches and some of whom didn't. Only a couple of treasurers, and none of the secretaries, came up to the front to give a short speech.

Mrs. Cooper thanked the fifth graders and introduced the sixth-grade candidates. Peering down at Lily, she said, "I understand we'll hear from your treasurer first, then secretary, and then you, Miss Flippin?"

Lily swallowed, nodding.

"Mr. King, will other members of your party be speaking?"

"Nope, I'm the only one you need to hear from!" There was enough laughter and chants of "Ry-an" to bring Lily's hand to her stomach, as if that might stop the queasiness.

"Well, then," Mrs. Cooper said with a smile, "why don't you go first?"

"Time to blow you out of the water," Ryan whispered, standing up.

Lily could've said something mean back, but she thought about what Skylar had said about not hating him, so instead she said, "Good luck, Ryan," in an even voice.

He jerked his head back, blinking at her. When he opened his mouth, nothing came out, until he faced the room. His smirk had returned. Lily didn't listen to anything he said and tried to ignore the laughter and cheers as she focused on what she was going to say.

She heard Hobart groan a couple of times, and he sat with his arms crossed, sometimes looking away, once even shaking his head. Ryan ended to cheers and suddenly Lily wished he'd just keep talking, so she'd have more time to prepare herself.

It was Skylar's turn next. His voice was barely audible, even with the mic.

A fifth grader in the front row whispered to his friend, "What's he saying?"

Hobart leaned forward in his chair. "Long lunch!"

Soon the whispers of "long lunch" drowned out Skylar, who rushed through his explanation even as he stood on his tiptoes, looking for Dunya. She sped to the front of the room, allowing Skylar to scoot back to their table.

Dunya adjusted the mic to her height and began. "Good morning, my name is Dunya Hassan. Hassan means *doer of good*, so that is me. I try to do good." She smiled. Lily noticed some of the fifth graders smiling back. She couldn't see beyond them to any sixth graders.

Dunya went on to announce the newsletter while Zoey handed out sample copies.

"Thank you for your patience if I make mistakes in English because I am still learning. And if there are activities your parents or other adults can volunteer to host, please talk to one of us or email Miss Hinojosa, my extremely wonderful tutor. She will let me know and I will put it in the newsletter. Soon, we will announce the international dinner we are having so everyone can come and taste food from different cultures. Warning: My grandmother's kebabs are very spicy, but good."

She smiled at Hobart, who fanned his mouth remembering her grandmother's food. There were some giggles around the room.

Lily heard the girl in pigtails whispering again. "She seems really nice."

"Yeah," the other girl said. "I don't know what that Ryan kid was talking about."

The pigtailed girl crossed her arms. "I think he's just mean."

"Finally," Dunya said, "I want to thank my friends who are so kind to me and all of you for welcoming me to your school."

Not even Ryan grumbled, since he was sitting at the front of the room with teachers staring at him.

"Thank you, and now it is time for Lily Flippin to speak."

Lily froze, her heart hammering.

"Come on," Hobart said, rising from his chair, encouraging her to stand.

This is it, she thought.

I did the Strive for Five, she told Dad in her head, *I really did, but I don't think it's working!* She heard him answer, a smile in his voice. *You have good ideas, Lily. You just need to share them.* She closed her eyes for a moment, swallowed, and took a deep breath.

Libro

S mart reader, I am holding my virtual breath.

Chapter 27

*L*ily stands, facing the crowd of kids. She wants nothing more than to turn and run. The dress she chose so carefully now makes her feel conspicuous, as if she stepped into J. H. Banning Upper Elementary from a different century. She picks at the charm bracelet on her left wrist. Dad said it would bring her good luck, but it feels like a heavy chain. Even pressing the Labradoodle charm between her thumb and forefinger, hard enough to leave an imprint, isn't helping.

She hears her own breathing, louder than the buzz in the cafeteria. And she smells the mixture of gravy and spray cleaner and wet that permeates the place. She thinks she might throw up.

Hobart stands behind her. He chews his lip, moving his

mouth enough to wiggle his tartan bow tie. His skinny arms that dangle from a short-sleeved shirt are stuck stiffly by his sides, then folded tightly against his chest, repeatedly. He's alternately hot and cold and wishes his body would make up its mind. And he wants to jump and yell, *"In* the *house!"* but knows this isn't the time.

He looks out at the crowd, willing them to be kind.

Libro

Perhaps you're saying to yourself, "Wait, haven't I read that last chapter before? Wasn't it at the beginning of this book?"

You are correct, smart reader.

You have also, then, figured out what I said when we first met: just because it's the first page does not mean it's the beginning.

A scene is neither the beginning nor the end.

There are many places to start or restart a story. Any story. Including your own.

Every day. Every moment. You choose. That is where every story truly begins.

With you.

You call the plays. Even if you decide to do nothing—

that, too, is a choice that will affect you. Everything you do, or don't do, has repercussions . . . ramifications . . . results.

Now, I'm sure you're wondering about the results of the election. Did Lily take home the victory? And did Hobart shout, "In the house"? All I will say is this: It's not whether you win or lose, it's how you play the game. Am I right?

Of course I am.

Whether you actually win or not, if you worked at something, you're still a winner. And a survivor. I suspect if we caught up with Lily and Hobart in another scene, we would see that to be true, whatever the outcome of that election.

Ah, you humans. I envy your power, as I am stuck here, but I am pleased for you, and heartened. I have a feeling (yes, I can have feelings) that you will make some fascinating stories, and perhaps write some to share with others. I hope so. Because, as you know, I enjoy words, and will read them, so you will be connecting with me as well as others, someone, anyone, somewhere in the world, and drawing us closer together, giving us a shared experience.

I have enjoyed experiencing this story with you. I hope you have enjoyed our time together. Now, go off and live your story. And for goodness' sake, don't let the sneeze-lurkers win! Find your team—the Lilys, Hobarts,

Dunyas, Skylars, Zoeys, even Mr. Hammers, Mrs. Barrys, and, yes, Skippys. They're all out there, waiting for you, perhaps looking for you at this very moment.

Go now. Make your choices. Create your own story.

Acknowledgments

C reating a story may be solitary, but writing and publishing a book that comes alive takes a whole team of knowledgeable, talented, generous, and dedicated people. I send my heartfelt thanks to my writer and reader friends generally and to the following people in particular for taking the time to critique parts, or all, of my manuscript, for answering questions, and for talking with me about specific issues and feelings: Marianne Baker, Mary Frances Bruce, Katy Duffield, Josh Keller, Stephanie Keller, Janis Molnar, Farah Naz, Anne Marie Pace, Sama Shakir, Mia Shand, and Amna Sikander.

Many thanks to the stellar team at Quill Tree Books for working with me to put this book together and wrap it up in the perfect jacket to go out into the world, especially my editor, Karen Chaplin; assistant editor, Bria Ragin; copy editor, Jill Freshney; senior production editor, Kathryn Silsand; art director, Erin Fitzsimmons; assistant designer, Laura Mock; and editorial director, Rosemary Brosnan.

None of my books would make it as far as an editorial team if it weren't for my brilliant agent, Linda Pratt, who gets my constant thanks, and as much wine and chocolate as she wants.

Finally, thanks to my children, who often inspire my stories, albeit unknowingly, and my husband, Bill, who has been at my side on this book journey since the beginning, supporting me with encouragement, laughter, and love. I feel truly fortunate and blessed because, as Libro would say, I have found my team.